A Wish on Gardenia Street

Also by Shelley Shepard Gray

Sisters of the Heart series
Hidden
Wanted
Forgiven
Grace

Seasons of Sugarcreek series
Winter's Awakening
Spring's Renewal
Autumn's Promise
Christmas in Sugarcreek

Families of Honor series
The Caregiver
The Protector
The Survivor
A Christmas for Katie (novella)

The Secrets of Crittenden County series
Missing
The Search
Found
Peace

The Days of Redemption series
Daybreak
Ray of Light
Eventide
Snowfall

Return to Sugarcreek series
Hopeful
Thankful
Joyful

Amish Brides of Pinecraft series
The Promise of Palm Grove
The Proposal at Siesta Key

Other books
Redemption

A Wish on Gardenia Street

AN AMISH BRIDES OF PINECRAFT NOVELLA

SHELLEY SHEPARD GRAY

AVON
INSPIRE
IMPULSE
An Imprint of HarperCollins Publishers

Excerpt from *A Wedding at the Orange Blossom Inn* copyright © 2015 by Shelley Shepard Gray.

Excerpt from *A Christmas Bride in Pinecraft* copyright © 2015 by Shelley Shepard Gray.

Illustrated map copyright © by Laura Hartman Maestro

EPub Edition JULY 2015 ISBN: 9780062422217

Print Edition ISBN: 9780062422224

10 9 8 7 6 5 4

Love is patient and kind.

1 CORINTHIANS 13:4

Don't worry about anything. Instead, pray about everything.

PHILIPPIANS 4:6

Most of us get experience when we are really looking for something else.

AMISH PROVERB

Illustrated map by

Phillipi

Serena River

Phillipi

N

U.S. POST OFFICE

The Quilt Haus

Carter Ave.
Pile Ave.
Tice Ave.

PINECRAFT PARK

Gilbert Ave.
Good Ave.
Kruppa Ave.
Miller Ave.
Graber Ave.
Yoder Ave.

Kaufman Ave.

Pinecraft Elementary School

Hacienda

Gardeni

Birky St.

YODER'S RESTAURANT

Hines Ave.

Estrada S

Cozy Cafe

Bimini St.

Frankie the beagle lives here

Wes

* Many of these locations are real, but like Serena the cat and Frank

Hartman Maestro

©2014

River

Orange
Blossom Inn

S. Beneva Rd.

Palm Grove
Mennonite Church

...e Sadler's
...se

...a

...hia Vista St.

Village
Pizza

Der
Dutchman
Restaurant

...craft
...mish
Church

Big Olaf
Creamery

Bus
Stop

PIONEER TRAILS

Clarinda St.

S. Beneva Rd.

Welcome
to
Pinecraft

Schrock St.

...to Siesta
Key

...e beagle, Shelley imagined a few, too

Chapter 1

June 10

EVERYTHING LOOKED THE same.

As she looked around the colorful, bright attic room of the Orange Blossom Inn, the very same room where she'd stayed just a few months ago, Mattie Miller felt a curious sense of déjà vu. The same bright quilts decorated the three twin beds. The same rag rugs warmed the wooden floor.

But yet everything was different.

This time, she wasn't going to be staying with Leona and Sara, her two best friends in the world. This time, she was going to be by herself. And instead of preparing to have the time of her life in their girlfriends' getaway, she was back in Pinecraft for Leona's wedding. Sara had planned to come, too. Unfortunately, she'd contracted pneumonia and their doctor had forbidden her to travel.

Therefore, Mattie had boarded the Pioneer Trails bus by herself and had passed the time on the twenty-hour journey with the company of a good book and a comfortable pillow and blanket. To her amazement, she'd slept for seven hours and had awoken with the sure feeling that everything was going to be amazing in Florida.

She just knew it.

Of course, it was going to be a special trip because she would get to watch Leona say her vows. But she had other plans, too. Other, secret plans she hadn't even dared to tell Leona.

Mattie Miller didn't intend to simply observe a romance. No, this time she was going to have a romance of her own.

During her visit in January, she and Danny Brenneman had grown fairly close. Since then, they'd exchanged a half-dozen letters. Though neither of them had declared anything, Mattie was positive that their friendship was ripe for blossoming into something more.

Yes, if all went well, she would be planning her wedding to Danny Brenneman soon. Just like her best friend, Leona. Before long, Mattie would be moving to Sarasota, too. She and Danny would have a perfect life together, and she and Leona would continue to be each other's best friend. They'd support each other through their first months of marriage, throw baby showers for each other, and raise their *kinner* together, too.

Just like they'd always planned.

And now, it was finally all going to happen.

"Are you sure you don't mind being up here in the attic all alone?" Beverly Overholt, the proprietor of the inn, asked, interrupting her drifting thoughts. "I feel badly that I had to switch you with the two ladies who were supposed to be staying in this room."

As long as she had a place to stay, Mattie didn't care where she slept. "I have two good legs, Miss Beverly. Stairs don't bother me. I don't think that lady can say the same."

"I imagine that is true." Smiling a bit sheepishly, Beverly added, "I canna tell you how surprised I was to see Mrs. Donaldson on crutches. One would have thought she'd have told me that she couldn't navigate stairs at the moment."

"I'm kind of happy to be in this big room, all by myself, actually. I share a room with my little sister at home." Running a hand over the lovely hand-stitched quilt, the very same one she'd slept under the last time she'd arrived, Mattie added, "Plus, being here brings back a lot of *gut* memories."

As she leaned against the door frame, Beverly's gaze warmed. "I imagine it does, dear. Having you here is going to bring back some fun memories for me, too."

"Truly?" Mattie was glad about that, but a bit surprised, too. Their previous visit hadn't been without a good share of drama.

"I have to admit to being a bit sad when you, Sara, and Leona got back on the Pioneer Trails bus. You girls, with your chattering and laughter, were a breath of fresh air. I enjoyed watching and listening to everything you were up to."

"You are remembering our visit a little too fondly, I think," Mattie quipped, recalling how she, Leona, and Sara had intended to have one last girls' weekend before Leona married Mattie's brother Edmund. They hadn't been in Pinecraft twenty-four hours before Leona had fallen in love with someone else—much to her and Sara's dismay. "We were full of drama, what with Leona falling in love with Zack. And then, of course, things only got worse when Edmund arrived unexpectedly." Grimacing slightly, she said, "I was afraid a fight was gonna break out in your gathering room!"

Beverly bit her bottom lip. "Yes, well . . ."

"We were also noisy and hungry, too," Mattie added with a smile. "I believe we attacked your tea every afternoon like locusts."

Beverly laughed. "I wouldn't say that, though I will make sure to feed you well this time, too. Are you sad that Sara couldn't come with you?"

"I really am. Sara was so upset when she realized she wasn't going to be able to make the wedding. We've all been close since we were little girls. But she's been so sick, I'm glad she's staying home. She needs to get better, not travel on a bus for twenty hours. I did, however, promise to tell her about everything that happens, so she'll be with us in spirit."

Stepping away from the doorway, Beverly smiled. "I'm sure you are anxious to see your girlfriend. I'll let you get unpacked so you can be on your way."

"Leona is supposed to meet me here. She and Zack had a meeting with Zack's Realtor so she couldn't meet the bus. But she'll be here soon."

Beverly crossed her arms over the bodice of her dark cranberry-colored dress. "I had forgotten that Zack and Leona were getting a house. That's nice."

Mattie nodded. "It's just down the road from his parents. All of them are excited about that." Leona had told her that Zack's parents had actually helped them buy the house, too. The Kaufmanns were a well-known family in Pinecraft and his father had a successful carpentry business.

"Is Zack working for his *daed* now?"

"Part time. He's also working for the bus company, too. They needed someone here to help the Amish tourists. He answers questions and acts as link between the Amish community and the rest of Sarasota. That way if someone gets sick or has a problem with their house or hotel, they have someone to go to that they can trust. Leona told me that he's doing a *gut* job there."

"I bet he is. Zack has always been especially helpful to everyone in the community."

"Leona is proud of him."

Beverly's striking green eyes warmed. "As she should be. Well, I'll send her up the minute she arrives then."

After Beverly closed the door, Mattie looked around the space again. The attic room held three beds, each decorated in bright shades of pink and purple. Two windows covered in sheer white curtains let in a wide expanse of light, brightening an already cheerful room. On one side of the room was a full bathroom, along with a small closet and some pegs on which to hang her dresses.

Then there was her favorite part of the room: a lovely window seat where she, Sara, and Leona had lounged and watched the world go by two stories below them.

Wanting to enjoy her first moments to the fullest, Mattie sat down on the cushion and gazed out at the people who walked by just in case she spied anyone she knew. Soon, however, it became apparent that her attention wasn't focused on the people but the bright day outside. The June sky was a clear blue, and it seemed as if every home and business owner on Gardenia Street had taken pains to grow the most beautiful flowers. Purple periwinkles, red geraniums, and pansies of every color imaginable decorated walks and pails and terra-cotta pots on most every front porch.

The neighbors across the way had out a lovely set of white wicker furniture. A lady and a fluffy white poodle were sitting on an oversized chair, looking so perfect it was as if they were posing for pictures.

Soon, with God's help, Mattie was sure that she, too, would be making her home here in sunny Sarasota. Maybe one day she'd have an expansive front porch, too. She could laze about with a good book while waiting for her husband to come home in the evenings. Later, they could sip on iced tea together as they watched the tourists pass by. Eventually she'd be taking care of her *kinner*, raising them under warm, sunny skies.

She was just about to drift into that vision when she saw Leona approaching the front walkway. Mattie tore out of the room, raced down the steps, and burst out of the front door just as Leona was about to knock.

"We're together again!" she cried as she gave Leona a fierce hug.

"I'm so happy to see you," Leona said as she wrapped her arms around her tightly.

"It feels like it's been forever instead of just weeks since we've seen each other."

Leona nodded. "Somehow the time seems longer when we're hundreds of miles apart."

As they turned and walked up the stairs, Mattie nodded. "I canna tell you the number of times I ached to tell you something but you haven't been around."

"At least you still have Sara."

"At least." However, Mattie wasn't sure what was going on with Sara anymore. Their last trip had put more distance between the three of them than mere miles. Sara now seemed more content to spend all her extra time reading, cooking, and sewing. She had also begun to volunteer at a local nursery for young children. All those things were pleasurable pursuits, to be sure. But they were far from Mattie's chosen list of fun activities.

Though Sara had no doubt not wanted to be sick, Mattie privately thought that she'd seemed rather relieved to have an excuse not to venture back down to Pinecraft.

When they reached the attic room, Leona looked around the room with a grin. "I canna believe Miss Beverly placed you up here again. And this time, you're all alone."

"Well, Sara was supposed to be here. Then Miss Beverly had a mix-up with one of the guests who is on crutches." Unable to resist teasing her, Mattie added, "But if you really feel sorry for me, you can share my room."

Leona smiled softly. "I just might do that."

"Truly?"

She nodded. "Though I am having fun staying in the

rental house with my parents, it's not the same as staying with you. Plus, I think I'm going to need to have at least a couple more nights as a single girl before I get married."

Mattie waved a hand around the room. "Feel free to stay as many nights as you'd like."

"*Danke.*"

Noticing how pink Leona's cheeks had become, she asked, "So, are you *neahfich* about the wedding?"

"I'm not nervous about marrying Zack at all," Leona said as she plopped down on one of the quilted twin beds. "I can't wait until we exchange our vows."

"I meant about everything else. Last time we talked, it sounded like you had a lot to do."

Leona grabbed one of the pillows and hugged it tightly. "Oh, there's *so* much to do. And every time I think I can relax for a few hours, my *mamm* and Zack's *mamm* come up with a new idea. It's exhausting, it is."

"I'm really glad I came here a full week before your wedding, then."

"Me too. I hope you really won't mind helping me with all the table runners and placemats."

"That's why I came, though we both know that I'm a better teacher than seamstress," Mattie said as she eyed the pretty stitches on the white quilt she was sitting on. No matter how hard she tried, she knew it was doubtful that she'd ever be able to stitch something so neatly.

"We're only going to be making table runners, not dresses. I think even you will be able to handle that just fine. Plus, my sisters and their husbands are arriving in four days. They'll be able to get anything finished that we need help with. However, I fear you're not going to have much time to sleep in and just relax."

"I wanted to help you prepare, not be entertained, silly. And to make sure you are okay. Are you okay?" Of course, the minute she uttered the question, Mattie knew it was a ridiculous one. Leona Weaver radiated happiness. Her blond hair was sun-streaked, her skin was lightly tanned against her bright pink short-sleeved dress, and she seemed to be wearing a permanent smile. Mattie felt pudgy, pale, and unkempt next to her.

"I am better than okay. I am happy. Zack is so wonderful. I can't wait to be his wife. I feel so blessed to know him." Still looking moony, Leona blushed. "You know, when I think about how different my life was a year ago back in Ohio, it makes my head spin."

"I can't believe I actually thought you should have married Edmund. You never looked this happy when you were by his side."

Instantly, Leona's smile faltered. "I'm sorry. I don't mean to sound as if I didn't appreciate your *bruder*. Edmund is a *gut* man."

"He is. But he was not the right man for you."

Looking a little uncomfortable, Leona asked, "Is he seeing anyone else now?"

Mattie nodded. "He's recently started courting Tillie Zook."

"Tillie?" Leona's eyebrows rose. "Now that seems like an odd pairing."

Mattie knew exactly what Leona wasn't saying. Tillie had a reputation for giving her opinion about everything and anything. And Edmund . . . well, Edmund was a man who liked his opinions best. Mattie would have never guessed that he would accept a woman who sometimes disagreed with him. "At first me and my *mamm* thought that, but they seem rather well suited. I think he needs a woman to challenge him from time to time."

"That is *gut* news." With a happy sigh, Leona kicked off her flip-flops and crossed her legs. Suddenly, she looked like a young teenager instead of a grown woman about to say vows. "Well, my *mamm* was right. Everything does happen for a reason. Now I am happy and Edmund is, too."

Mattie smiled and tried to look pleased for her best friend in the whole world—but it was hard. In the last year, Leona had gone from being one man's fiancée to embarking on a whirlwind courtship with one of the nicest men Mattie had ever met.

All the while, Mattie had been trying to figure out what was going to happen between her and Danny. She had met Danny the same afternoon Leona had met Zack. But that was where the similarities of their courtships ended. While Leona and Zack had fallen swiftly in love, she and Danny had simply become good friends.

When she, Sara, and Leona had gone back to Ohio, Mattie and Danny had exchanged a few letters but nothing meaningful. Unfortunately, though Danny had written that he was looking forward to seeing her, she wasn't sure if he was as eager to begin a real relationship as she was.

Leona suddenly looked uneasy. "Um, is staying here okay? I know when we first talked, I said that you and

Sara could probably stay at Zack's parents' *haus*. I'm worried you're going to use all your savings."

Though at first Mattie had worried about the cost, her parents had surprised her by offering to pay for her room. "It's fine. It's more than fine, because my parents are helping me out," she said as she stretched out on her bed. "Plus, it's filled with so many wonderful memories that just sitting in this bright room makes me happy."

Besides, Mattie was starting to think that she might need some space, too. She was anxious and nervous about the prospect of seeing Danny again. If things didn't go as she'd planned, she had a feeling that she might need some quiet time to reflect on her future.

Leona suddenly smiled. "I'm so glad you did come. I've been anxious to hear about everything you are doing. Has any boy caught your eye back home?"

Mattie was about to confide that she was anxious to see Danny when they were interrupted by a clatter downstairs, followed by the rush of footsteps on the stairs.

"Leona?" a deep voice called. "Leona, are you up there?"

Looking alarmed, Leona jumped to her feet, grabbed her flip-flops in one hand, and ran out to the landing. "I'm in the attic, Zack," she called before starting down the two flights of stairs.

After grabbing her purse and locking her room, Mattie followed. She was very curious about what could have made Zack come looking for Leona less than thirty minutes after she'd arrived.

It was time to go find out.

Chapter 2

In a panic, Leona rushed down the stairs, hardly aware of anything or anyone. She only had eyes for Zack, who was standing rigidly just inside the inn's foyer, his light tan straw hat clutched in his hands. His light brown hair was rumpled, as if he'd run his fingers through it several times, and his blue eyes were filled with worry, too. The dimple that she loved so much when he smiled was in hiding.

All in all, he looked completely different from his usual, easygoing self. Thinking of all their wedding preparations—as well as his little sister Effie, who was still wearing a cast on her broken leg—Leona knew there were a dozen things that could have made him so upset.

The moment she reached his side, he reached for her hand. "I'm glad I found you," he murmured.

"Me too. What is wrong? What happened?"

Just as he was about to respond, he looked beyond her.

"Hey, Mattie," he said around a slight smile. "Welcome back."

"*Danke.* I'm glad to be here."

Leona had never considered herself to be an impatient girl, but these last few minutes were driving her crazy. "Zachary. What is going on?"

He squeezed her hand. "I'm sorry. I didn't mean to scare you."

"Zack, what happened?"

"I was just over at Winnie Sadler's house. I was going to mow her yard for her, but when I knocked on her door to tell her I was there, I discovered she was in quite a state. Serena is missing and she's frantic."

Mattie frowned. "I thought Serena was her cat."

"It is."

Leona didn't know whether to chide Zack for getting her so upset or to start laughing. She settled for gently reminding him who and what they were talking about. "That cat always runs off. And Mrs. Sadler is always certain she is never going to come back. I'm sure she'll turn up in a few hours like she always does."

"This is different, Le. She hasn't seen Serena since yesterday morning. She's worried sick. When I left her *haus*, Mrs. Sadler was literally in tears." Looking apologetic, he shifted from one foot to the other. "I know you two are anxious to catch up, and it is just a cat, but is there any way you two could catch up while looking after Mrs. Sadler?"

"What do you need us to do, Zack?" Mattie asked.

"Just sit with her for an hour or two while I try and

find her cat? Maybe help her heat up some soup or make a sandwich or something?"

Leona bit her lip. Of course she wanted to help Mrs. Sadler. Though she was elderly and in frail health, she did pretty well on her own. Still, much of her ability to live independently had to do with Zack's constant checkups.

But Mattie had just arrived and it seemed like a terribly selfish gesture to ask her best friend to come sit with a crying elderly lady who was missing her cat.

"Mattie, I'm so sorry. I need to go help Zack with Mrs. Sadler. But you can stay here and rest. I'll stop by when things settle down." Thinking of how chaotic things were already, she rolled her eyes. "If they ever settle down."

Mattie's gaze was filled with sympathy—and a good trace of amusement. "You mean *we* need to go help Mrs. Sadler."

"You don't mind?"

She shook her head. "I came to Pinecraft to spend time with you. I don't care what we're doing as long as we're together."

Leona was beyond relieved. "You, Mattie Miller, are a *wonderful-gut* friend."

"I know. You know what? Let me go freshen up for a moment, then I'll be ready to go. I'll be back downstairs in five minutes."

"*Danke*, Mattie," Zack said. "I'm sorry to ruin your first day here."

She waved a hand. "It's not ruined, Zack. I'm perfectly happy to help."

After Mattie trotted back inside, Zack stepped close.

"Thank you for understanding, Leona," he murmured. "I know this doesn't seem too important but it is to Mrs. Sadler."

"I'm glad you asked for my help."

"I came over without giving it much thought," he said, as his expression softened. "I simply knew I could count on you."

As he ran a finger along her jawline, Leona trembled. All it took was a warm smile or a sweet touch for her to melt in his arms. "You can always count on me. Always." She smiled back at him.

After glancing around, obviously to make sure they were alone, Zack kissed her cheek. And with the briefest of pauses, he brushed his lips across hers.

Though it was a chaste kiss, it was also a surprise. Feeling her cheeks heat, she teased him. "Zack, look at you, kissing me in the entryway of the Orange Blossom Inn."

He smiled mischievously. "I know I shouldn't be so bold, but I canna help myself. I've missed you. Plus, with Mattie in town and a cat on the loose, there's no telling when I'll get another chance."

He had a good point. They were bound to get busier and busier now that it was the final week before the wedding. When her sisters arrived, she doubted she'd have any time at all to spend with her fiancé.

Leona was just about to lean in and kiss his cheek back when she heard voices coming from the front gathering room and steps on the staircase behind them. Belatedly, she realized that Mattie had only shut the screen door, not the main one. She stepped away and attempted to look less like an impatient bride-to-be.

"Don't stop on my account," Mattie called out from the landing.

"Or mine," Beverly teased as she entered the room. "I think you two are adorable."

To Leona's amusement, Zack turned bright red. "I think it's time we left."

After smiling at Beverly, Leona linked arms with Mattie and followed. Yes, they were busy. And now they had to look for a silly cat, too.

But everything was still *gut*. It was actually pretty perfect.

FORTY MINUTES LATER, Leona and Mattie were walking down Hines Avenue with Zack again. After they'd attempted to sit with Mrs. Sadler, it had become obvious that the lady would rather have them search. When Leona had heard Zack a few houses away, she and Mattie went to join him.

At first he'd seemed happy for their help, but now he was looking at her worriedly again. "Are you sure you're not upset with me for ruining your reunion with Mattie?"

"I'm sure." She was dismayed with the situation, but not with him.

"Sure?"

"Of course. Mrs. Sadler has been so sweet to me; I want to help her if I can." Darting a quick look at Mattie, who was now trailing behind in a not-so-obvious attempt to let Leona and Zack have a few minutes of privacy, she whispered, "I just hope Mattie doesn't get mad at me. She didn't come here to be dragged around Pinecraft, searching for lost cats."

"She seemed to understand."

"I hope so. Do you think Serena's disappearance is anything to be worried about?"

"I doubt it. For years, that cat has done whatever she's wanted to do, regardless of how much Mrs. Sadler attempts to coddle her."

"People do say that cats pick their owners, not the other way around. I would have thought Mrs. Sadler would be used to Serena running off by now."

Staring straight ahead, Zack continued. "Mrs. S seems a little more sensitive than usual. Something is going on with her, I'm not sure what. And, well, it isn't like that cat not to return for supper. That's something new."

"I hope nothing happened to her. Mrs. Sadler will be devastated!"

"I agree. I just hope we find her soon. You and I have a new house to move into and we're getting married in eight days. This is the last thing we need to be doing."

Though she'd been thinking much the same thing, hearing the concern in Zack's voice made her reflective. "Who knows? Maybe the Lord decided that it was time I focused on something besides my own concerns."

"Maybe that's why Mattie is here, so you can focus on her concerns."

She lowered her voice. "I don't know what you're talking about."

His blue eyes were fairly dancing. "Danny told me that they've been exchanging letters. Do you think something is brewing between them?"

She pressed a hand to his arm. "Is Danny looking forward to seeing her again?"

"He seems eager, but I don't know for sure. Do you want me to ask him when he and I are out looking for that cat?"

He was so dear. She knew he was seeking to lighten her mood. But she also saw that those blue eyes of his looked tired. Poor Zack! He was trying to be everything to everyone. If she didn't step in, he was going to be exhausted. "You don't have to do that. I'll see what I can find out from Mattie first."

"*Danke*, Leona."

After smiling at him again, she paused so Mattie could catch up. "I'm really hoping that this won't take too long."

"Stop worrying about me, Le. I'm fine." Just as she was about to say something else, Mattie gasped. "Isn't that Danny?"

"*Jah*," Zack answered. "He was going to help me with Mrs. Sadler's yard work but he had a couple of chores to finish first. Looking at Mattie more closely, he asked, "You don't mind seeing Danny, do ya?"

"*Nee*. Not at all."

Leona bit her lip so she wouldn't giggle. Mattie was now smiling from ear to ear.

As Leona looked from Danny to Mattie, she realized that Zack had been right. Now she had something mighty important to focus on besides herself—a blossoming romance between Mattie and one of Zack's best friends.

THIS WAS DEFINITELY not how Mattie had imagined seeing Danny for the first time in months. Looking down at her dove gray dress, she wished she'd taken the time to at least change into a more flattering color. This was her favorite traveling dress, but it was about three years old, and a remnant from an eight-month period when she'd gone a little crazy eating baked goods from the Sugarcreek Inn.

After one of her sisters had teased her about looking much like one of the squirrels in their tree—slim up top but decidedly heavy around the midsection—she'd begun replacing her daily baked treat with an apple.

In six months' time, most of her dresses had had to be taken in, but she'd kept this one on the off chance that she'd need a loose-fitting dress from time to time. Therefore, it was exceptionally comfortable. It was also exceptionally unflattering.

Oh, but she *really* wished she'd taken the time to change!

Since Zack had picked up his pace and was already talking to Danny, Leona had returned to her side. "Now it's my turn to ask about nerves," she teased. "Are you nervous about seeing Danny again?"

"Truth?"

"*Jah.*"

She nodded, deciding that she was going to need as

much help from Leona as possible not to mess up this reunion with Danny. "We've shared a couple of letters, but I'm not sure if they meant as much to him as they did to me. Have you heard anything?"

"No, but Danny wouldn't have told me a thing. He would have told Zack."

"So has he told Zack anything about me?" she asked impatiently, hardly able to tear her gaze away from the two men.

Leona visibly fought a smile. "*Nee*. But, ah, you know how men are. They don't like to talk about relationships like women do."

Mattie wasn't so sure about that. Though she had never actually been in a serious relationship before, she'd heard Edmund talk about his frustrations with Leona both while they were courting and after they'd broken up. She had also heard her older sister and her brother-in-law talk about things, too.

Perhaps it wasn't that Danny didn't talk about relationships and romance. Rather, perhaps he just wasn't interested in her!

Her heart sank. Though her mother had warned her not to get her hopes up too high, it seemed that she already had. She wanted to be in love. She wanted someone to love her—someone fun and cute and personable like Danny. She wanted what Leona had. That acknowledgment dismayed her and made her feel utterly selfish. She knew it wasn't right to be thinking about herself, especially not at a time like this, when Leona needed to concentrate on her wedding.

Plus, they had a cat to find.

"Don't worry about me and Danny," she said quickly. "Whatever is meant to happen will happen, and I will be glad for that, too." It wasn't quite how she felt, but it was all she was willing to say out loud.

"That's a terrific attitude to have. I'm impressed."

"Don't be too impressed. There's just nothing to worry about at the moment."

Leona hesitated, then blurted, "This sounds sappy, but I hate being so happy when you seem so sad."

Mattie couldn't help but grin. Leona didn't sound sappy, she sounded like Leona. "I'm not sad and I'm not unhappy. I promise, I am fine. I'm simply wishing for things that might not happen. Everyone does that, I think. Even me."

Luckily, there was no more time to talk about things because Danny was walking toward her with a smile on his face. He had on a pale green shirt, loose black pants, and black leather flip-flops. He was tan and handsome and, best of all, he was smiling directly at her.

"Mattie, hello! This is a *gut* surprise!"

His greeting was perfect! Everything she'd wished for. "*Jah*," she replied, knowing she sounded more than a little breathless but unable to help herself. "I arrived this morning on the bus."

"That is *wonderful-gut* news. I had forgotten that you would be arriving today."

That comment, on the other hand, was not so perfect.

"I wrote you what day I was going to arrive."

"Did you?" He rubbed his chin. "I guess I forgot."

As her spirits sank, Zack came to her rescue. "You two are going to have to have your reunion another time. We've got to find that cat. If we don't, Mrs. Sadler is going to make herself sick."

"That cat will turn up. She always does," Danny said.

"If she doesn't, I don't know what Mrs. Sadler is going to do."

"I do," Leona said with a shake of her head. "She's going to make you unable to think about anything else but Serena."

"Leona's right," Danny said. "Mrs. Sadler is a nice lady, but she won't care that you've got a wedding to plan. She'll make sure you know she's miserable."

"Come on, Mattie," Leona said as she started toward the house with a determined expression on her face. "Let's stop by again. Zack, work your magic and find that cat."

"Will do." Turning to Danny, Zack said, "Let's try the cat's usual places."

"Want to start with the trees in front of Palm Grove Church?"

"Yep. We've got to find that darn cat, the sooner the better."

"See ya, Mattie," Danny called out before walking away with Zack.

Mattie raised her hand to wave good-bye before realizing that he wouldn't see her. His back was to her and he was already deep in conversation with Zack.

"He *forgot* that I was coming today," she said as they made their way up Mrs. Sadler's driveway.

"Don't take his words to mean anything but the truth.

As I've said, everything has been pretty crazy around here." Leona looped her arm through Mattie's. "And hey, at least you got to see him."

"That is true."

There was no time to worry about Danny's less than enthusiastic greeting once they entered Mrs. Sadler's house. After thanking them for coming with a tremulous smile, the elderly lady sat down in her rocking chair. "Is Zachary out looking?"

"*Jah*, and Danny is with him."

"Oh, *gut*." Worrying her bottom lip, she said, "I simply don't know where Serena is."

Leona took a seat beside Mattie on the worn tan couch. "Zack will find her, Mrs. Sadler. You know him. He can do anything."

"I have a bad feeling about this, though."

"Remember that verse from Philippians? The Scripture says, 'Don't worry about anything. Instead pray about everything.'"

"Those are words to remember for sure," Mrs. Sadler said, "but I just am not sure if the Lord is particularly worried about my Serena."

"I tell my students all the time that the Lord cares about each one of us and our concerns," Mattie said. "I'd like to think that I was telling the truth."

"I hope you are right," Mrs. Sadler said with a worried frown. "That little cat is my best friend. I simply don't know what I'm going to do if she is gone forever."

As she exchanged a look with Leona, Mattie hoped and prayed they wouldn't find out.

Chapter 3

June 11

It was noon. Mattie had slept past breakfast. Maybe even lunch, too.

Feeling bleary and much like she'd been run over by one of the Pioneer Trails buses, Mattie closed her eyes again. She was tempted to roll over and doze a few more hours in her exceptionally comfortable bed. Miss Beverly had told her once that she'd upgraded all of the inn's linens to higher thread counts and purchased brand-new down pillows a few years ago.

Though Mattie would never tell her mother, her bed at the top of the Orange Blossom Inn was the most comfortable one she'd ever slept in.

After reminding herself that she would be able to return to her cozy nest that very night, she at last crawled out and slipped on her robe. A glance out the window confirmed that the day was sunny and bright.

Yes, it really was time to take a shower and get dressed. However, all she wanted to do was find some coffee and figure out what to do next.

Yesterday had to be considered a wash. She'd spent the majority of her time consoling Mrs. Sadler and helping Zack's mother organize her kitchen so everyone could start cooking the wedding meal in earnest. She and Leona had been so tired that they'd agreed to have sleepover another night. All either of them wanted to do was get some rest.

As she brushed her long hair, Mattie realized that even though she'd been mighty busy, she'd also spent very little time with Danny. In fact, he'd kind of acted like he was trying to avoid her. But she was probably imagining that.

But what if she wasn't?

Luckily, a light tapping interrupted her thoughts. "Mattie? It's Beverly. Are you still here?"

She ran across the room and opened her door. When she saw that Miss Beverly was holding a carafe of coffee and a mug in her hands, she almost hugged her. "Bless you! You brought me *kaffi*!"

"I did. Tricia's coming up in a minute with some apricot scones and some granola and yogurt, too."

Remembering that Tricia was Beverly's niece who'd come for an extended visit, Mattie smiled. "This is so sweet of you. *Danke*."

"It's no trouble," Beverly said as she walked into the room and set everything on the desk. "You looked exhausted last night. Ah, here's Tricia."

"Good afternoon, sleepyhead," Tricia said with an infectious smile. She was Mattie's age and had a bubbly, effervescent personality. They'd immediately hit it off.

"Aunt Bev and I decided if you weren't coming down to the food, we'd best bring it up to you."

"Tricia, you and your aunt are now my favorite people in the world."

Tricia grinned. "Only because I'm not making you look for that silly cat."

"When I heard how long Zack and Danny looked yesterday, I couldn't believe it," Beverly said.

"I wasn't going to say anything, but don't you think everyone is overreacting a bit?" Mattie asked.

Beverly shrugged. "Mrs. Sadler is such a dear lady. She's very kind. But, um, well, she can be rather single-minded, too. It's in everyone's best interest to find that cat. She won't give anyone a moment's peace otherwise. Oh, I'm supposed to tell you that Leona and Zack stopped by about three hours ago."

"Three hours ago?"

"After they heard you were still sleeping, Leona wanted you to know that she was going out to breakfast with Zack," Tricia supplied. "She said to tell you that she'd be back at two to take you to The Quilt Haus."

"Oh, yes," Mattie remembered. "We're going to pick out fabric for the placemats and table runners. I'll be ready long before two."

Giving her a sympathetic look, Beverly said, "Try to pace yourself, dear."

"Even if you slept on the bus, I think it still takes a day or two to recover from the journey," Tricia said.

"It takes some time to adjust to new surroundings," Beverly said. "Give yourself that time." After pouring

Mattie a cup of coffee, she added, "Enjoy your breakfast, dear."

Mattie was about to say that she was not feeling any lasting effects from the trip when it suddenly occurred to her that maybe Beverly wasn't only speaking about the bus ride. Instead, she smiled wanly and sipped slowly.

When she was alone again, Mattie couldn't help but think that Beverly might have been right. Things were about to change with her and Leona. While she was excited for Leona's new journey with Zack, Mattie realized she was also a little sad that things between them would now be different. Leona would be a married woman while Mattie was still hoping for a serious beau.

It was time to relax and remind herself that everything would happen in the right time. In the Lord's time. That wasn't always an easy thing to remember but it was certainly worth reflecting upon.

Two hours later, she was standing outside on the inn's wide front porch dressed in a short-sleeved dark pink dress and a new pair of flip-flops. Though it was warm in Walnut Creek in June, she rarely wore flip-flops when she was out and about. Instead, she had a pair of lightweight tennis shoes. They were good for walking and were comfortable, too.

But they didn't allow the freedom that sandals did.

She was just wondering when she would have an excuse to buy several more pairs when Leona approached.

"How are you feeling today, Mattie? Did you catch up on your sleep?"

"I slept so late! I heard you stopped by earlier. I'm sorry I missed you."

"There's no reason to apologize. I never get enough sleep on the bus. I shouldn't have kept you so busy yesterday."

"I'm fine now and ready to get busy." She clasped her hands together. "Now, where are we going first?"

"The Quilt Haus. I wanted you to help me pick fabric for everything we talked about."

"Lead the way."

Looking delighted about their trip to the fabric store and the project they had to do, Leona practically raced down the inn's front steps. Following far more sedately behind her, Mattie couldn't help but notice all the changes that had taken place.

It used to be Mattie who had talked nonstop and rushed to do things. Now it looked like their places had been exchanged. Leona was now mighty pleased about everything, and more importantly, she seemed both relaxed and at peace with herself; the complete opposite of how Mattie was feeling. Leona also looked different. She now carried herself with a bit more confidence. Her pretty brown eyes were bright and a constant smile played on her lips. She was lightly tanned and no longer looked the slightest bit awkward walking down the sidewalk in rubber flip-flops. In short, she looked like a woman who fit in perfectly in Pinecraft and was pleased with her life.

It was so different from how Mattie felt.

For a moment, Mattie considered confiding in Leona how worried she was about her future. But she firmly pushed that aside. She had not come to Pinecraft to complain or to hoist her problems on Leona's shoulders.

Resolutely, she concentrated on taking in all the sights Leona showed her. Pinecraft was as darling as ever. Because it wasn't as crowded as it had been in February, Mattie was able to look with ease at the windows of different shops they passed.

As they walked along the streets, Mattie noticed that just like last time, most girls their age wore brightly colored short-sleeved dresses in every color of the rainbow. Half of them wore sunglasses, too. Most everyone was wearing bright-colored flip-flops, and a couple of men and women were walking barefoot, just as if they were strolling along the beach.

Though at this time of year it wasn't much of a transition to adjust to the Florida warmth from Ohio, Mattie decided that the air certainly did feel different. There was a different type of energy in the air, too. People seemed more relaxed. Things moved at a slower pace.

"You're walking pretty slowly. Is the heat getting to you already?" Leona teased.

"*Nee*. I was just thinking to myself that while it's warm back in Walnut Creek, too, things feel different here."

"I agree. Even though Zack tells me that this is the slow season, I think things move a bit more slowly here all year long. Maybe it's because we're in the South," Leona mused as they passed a group of English children. They were scampering around together, and two of them held little bright-colored bottles from the dollar store and were blowing soap bubbles. "They are so cute."

"I'm kind a surprised to see so many *kinner* here in the middle of summer."

"There are lots of *kinner* here on their summer breaks." Looking a bit dreamy, Leona added, "I told Zack I don't think I'll ever get used to enjoying warm weather during all twelve months of the year . . . but I aim to try."

"I don't think that would be a difficult thing to get used to," Mattie said, already dreading fall and winter.

Looking a bit mischievous, Leona said, "You better watch out, Mattie. If you're not careful, you might end up liking Florida life so much you won't want to leave."

That, of course, was what she'd been secretly hoping. In addition to helping with Leona's wedding, she wanted to get to know Danny better. Then, if things did progress, why, one day she could live here, too.

That would be wonderful. But, of course, right now it was simply a hope and a dream. "I know I'm going to have a hard time leaving you again," she said. "I've missed you these last couple of months."

"I've missed you, too. I'm really glad you came down here for a spell."

"Me too." She felt as if she was on the verge of breaking down into tears.

Leona waved a hand in front of her own face. "We have to stop talking about how much we miss each other. If we continue on that path, I'm going to start crying."

"Let's not do that."

"Agreed," she said as they stopped in front of The Quilt Haus. "Here we are."

When they entered, Mattie was immediately struck

by how cool, dark, and quiet the place was compared to the warmth and brilliant colors of the street. In the back, a lone woman in her fifties was carefully quilting a simple building block pattern.

Leona weaved her way through several tables laden with bolts of fabric until she was standing directly in front of the woman. "Hello, Meg," she said politely. "This is my friend Mattie. She just arrived from Walnut Creek."

Meg slowly lifted her head, eyed Mattie like she was ruining her day, and muttered, "Need anything, Leona?"

"Not yet. We're going to look around for now."

Meg didn't deign to answer. Instead, she quietly went back to work, her needle darting in and out of the quilt's fabric without stopping.

To Mattie's surprise, Leona didn't look the least bit offended by the woman's reserved manner. Instead, she smiled as she made her way back to Mattie's side before grabbing her hand and pulling her to a shelf stuffed full with bolts of blue fabric.

"Is she always like that?" Mattie whispered.

"Pretty much." Keeping her voice low, Leona added, "I know she's gruff, but I think it's just her nature. You'll get used to it." As if Leona had noticed that Mattie didn't seem all that enthused, she looked at her nervously. "So, um, what do you think? Isn't this place darling?"

"It is." She was only trying to be nice, however. Truthfully, The Quilt Haus looked like any other fabric store she'd ever been in, except that it was a little smaller, was a whole lot less crowded, and was presided over by a sourpuss.

"I was thinking of making everything from just four shades of blue. What do you think?"

"I think it sounds perfect."

"Which shades, though?" Leona nibbled her bottom lip as she gazed at each section of fabric. "I think there are almost a dozen to choose from."

There were a lot of shades. Too many to differentiate between in the dimly lit room. "I don't know which ones would be best. You choose."

"But you have the better eye for color, Mattie."

Mattie didn't think so—Sara was the one who worked in a fabric store in Berlin—but she would certainly give it her best shot. "Why don't you show me which ones you fancy and we'll go from there?"

Leona nodded as she picked up one bolt, then another. "Do you want to work on a project of your own? We could get you some fabric today, too."

"I came here to help you, Le."

"I know. While I appreciate all of your help, I don't mind if you make something for yourself. Perhaps you could make a table runner for someone."

Mattie didn't want to be mean, but she had no desire to spend her extra time on a project for herself. "I don't know who I would give a table runner to."

"You could make it for the quilt auction," Meg blurted, her deep voice practically echoing through the small space. "Or give it to someone in need. That's the right thing to do."

Mattie believed in giving to the needy, she really did, but she didn't have any desire to work on a project at the moment. She felt bad enough that she had come to Florida not just for Leona's wedding but to see Danny, too. If she did end up spending time with Danny as she hoped to, Mattie was pretty certain she wouldn't have any extra time to be making crafts and quilts for other people. She was going to be busy falling in love and making plans of her own.

"Leona, why don't you get your fabric now? Then we can get on our way."

She frowned. "You already want to leave? But we just got here."

Practically feeling Meg's glare resting malevolently on her back, Mattie decided a white lie was in order. "We've got a lot of placemats to make and only a couple of days to do it. I'm anxious to get started."

"Oh!" Leona turned contrite. "Of course. Let me pay for this, then we'll get some lunch. And then we can get busy on the placemats."

"Sounds like a plan."

Twenty minutes later, they were in line at Yoder's, the famous Amish restaurant located in the heart of Pinecraft. The line was long, but Mattie now knew it was always long. Most people who dined there expected to stand in line for at least forty minutes before being directed to a table.

"So, care to tell me why you were so anxious to get out of the fabric store?" Leona asked.

"It's nothing."

"Mattie. We both know that isn't true."

"Well, besides the fact that Meg didn't act all that fond

of our company, I'm kinda worried about seeing Danny again."

Leona chuckled. "You're right about Meg. She doesn't make the best first impression."

"Or second."

"I'll give you that. She is who she is," she said with a shrug of her shoulders. "Now, why don't you tell me about Danny. Why are you worried about spending time with him?"

Mattie knew it was time to be a little more forthcoming. Feeling her cheeks heat, she blurted, "I really like him."

"He likes you, too."

"*Nee*, I mean, I *really* like him. I like him the way you like Zack."

Leona's brown eyes widened. "Oh."

Mattie's spirits sank. She'd been secretly hoping that Danny had shared something similar with Zack, and thus, Leona. "I was hoping that he would be more eager to see me." She'd even imagined he might meet her bus when it arrived!

"He seemed happy to see you last night."

"*Nee*, he was friendly last night."

Leona raised her eyebrows. "Is there a difference?"

"I think so. I mean, there we were, all together at Mr. and Mrs. Kaufmann's house . . ."

"So?"

"Leona, Danny and I hadn't seen each other in months, but we have been writing to each other. I guess I was hoping he'd want to spend some time alone with me."

"We were all playing cards . . ."

Mattie appreciated her friend's attempts to make her feel better, she really did. But Danny's lack of interest had been fairly obvious. "He didn't even try."

"Danny has a lot of sisters, Mattie. He might not be used to thinking of girls in a romantic way."

As far as excuses went, Mattie figured that was a pretty bad one. "That makes no sense at all."

Leona sighed. "I suppose it doesn't." After a pause, she said, "Zack didn't want me to say anything, but he did say that Danny told him you two have been writing to each other. If he mentioned those letters, they must have made an impression on him."

"That's something, I suppose."

"I know! Tonight, I'll ask Zack to ask Danny how he feels about you."

That, Mattie was sure, was a recipe for disaster. There was a good possibility that Zack would be blunt, Danny would feel awkward, and then she would be embarrassed. To make matters worse, she'd have to see all of them for the next week. Quickly, she said, "*Nee*, don't do that. I'll figure things out myself."

"It's no trouble. When Zack gets off work he and Danny are going to go out looking for Serena again. I'll have him ask Danny about you in a casual way when they are out looking for that darn cat."

"Really, don't." Mattie didn't know a lot about dating and courting, but she knew enough to understand that getting Leona's future husband involved was not going to make things easier. Taking a deep breath, she made a decision. "Leona, if Danny and I are ever going to have a real relationship, I need to learn to simply talk to him on my own."

"You sure?"

"Absolutely!"

"Okay then," Leona said as the hostess picked up two menus and led them to a table near the front windows. "Let's concentrate on getting some lunch, then get ready to sew."

"Don't forget, we need some pie, too." If there was ever a day for a thick slice of Yoder's key lime pie, this was it.

Chapter 4

June 12

MATTIE SMOOTHED THE bright blue fabric in her lap. She'd just completed her second placemat, and it had taken only half the time of the first one. That was a relief. For a moment, there, she'd thought she was going to have to tell Leona there was no way they were going to have all twenty-four placemats done in time for the wedding reception. But now she was pretty sure she would have no problem getting them completed.

And maybe that was a good thing, too, since yet another day had passed without more than the briefest exchanges of conversation with Danny.

Thankful she was sitting alone, she leaned her head back against the cushions of the couch and sighed.

Danny Brenneman was turning out to be extremely elusive.

Though she'd always been teased about her tendency to wear her heart on her sleeve, Mattie was grateful for the trait. She'd been more than obvious in her letters with Danny that she'd hoped their casual correspondence was the beginning of something more. And because he'd kept writing back, she'd hoped that he wanted the same thing.

It was embarrassing to realize that he'd probably only been writing her because she was his best friend's fiancée's best friend.

After taking a fortifying sip of iced tea, she scanned the room, enjoying how the couch was a perfect match to the raspberry-colored easy chair to her right, the white wicker rocking chair with the lemon yellow cushions across from her, and the whitewashed oversized coffee table resting in the middle of the room. The bright, bold color scheme screamed Florida, and the moment Mattie had seen it, she'd declared that she'd never seen a prettier room.

After lunch, they'd settled into the back sunroom of the house Leona's parents had rented for the wedding and spent the afternoon sewing. It was an afternoon straight out of their past, only better because they weren't dodging either of their mothers or a constant long list of chores.

For almost the first time since she'd arrived, Mattie was feeling content. Leona was, too, if the four-foot-long table runner she'd just pieced together was any indication.

Setting her placemats to one side, Mattie picked up the table runner. At first glance, the various triangles had looked hopelessly mismatched, but the end result was beyond pretty. All the triangles were in various shades of blue and reminded Mattie how the colors of the ocean seemed to blend together when the light hit the water just right.

"Are you looking for mistakes?" Leona teased as she entered the room.

"Not at all. I was just sitting here thinking that you have a gift with design. You could sell this if you wanted, Le."

Leona smiled as she sat down in the yellow chair. "Maybe one day I'll do something like that. It would be a fun job for me. I'll ask Meg at The Quilt Haus what she thinks about that."

Mattie groaned. "I hope she'll be supportive and not cranky."

"I promise that she's nicer than she seemed. I don't know why, but she's awfully reserved with strangers."

"Then she's taken up the wrong occupation, don'tcha think? Most of her customers are likely strangers."

Leona giggled. "I suppose you have a point. She does have a nice shop, though. All of us locals love it."

"This place really has become your home, hasn't it?"

"It has. I'm happy here. Everyone has made me feel welcome, and of course, I'm blessed to have Zack."

"He is a *gut* man."

"He is. He loves me, and he's gone out of his way to introduce me to everyone he knows."

"That says a lot, since it seems like he knows everyone."

"That is true. In many ways I feel like his family is the heart of Pinecraft, at least the Pinecraft that I know. The Kaufmanns have made sure to let everyone know that I'm now a part of their family. Because of that, everyone in their circle has gone out of their way to make me feel welcome, too."

"The Kaufmanns are really nice. I like his siblings,

too." Thinking about the night before, when they'd all gone over to Zack's parents' house for cards, she added, "I saw last night how much Effie has grown to love you."

Leona's expression softened. "I love her, too. She's such a sweet girl. She's really helped me become a part of Zack's family. Every time I'm around her, she's reached out to me. She really has a good heart."

"I wish I had been that way at her age. I remember being pretty self-centered."

"You weren't. You were just outspoken."

Mattie chuckled. "That's one way to put it. I think my sisters called me loud and gregarious."

"I've always liked that about you." Leona shrugged. "Every child has to grow into herself, I think. Your gregariousness made me want to be near you. Effie's physical challenges have melted away some of her shyness, at least when she's around adults."

"Maybe so. Or maybe her shyness has lessened because of how well she's doing. She seems to be getting around pretty well."

Leona nodded. "She's tough, that's for sure. I can never get over about how little she complains. Zack said he's pretty sure Effie is always in more pain than she lets on. I worry that she's going to overdo it."

"I'm sure Zack and his siblings will keep an eye on her. They seem protective."

"They are." Leona smiled as she pulled her needle through the fabric again. "Plus, she has a new friend who seems to be rather interested in her welfare."

"Oh?"

"She confided to me that a popular boy at school has become a good friend. He walks with her in the halls."

Mattie put her project back down on her lap. "She just turned thirteen, right?" When Leona nodded, she said, "Maybe this friendship will blossom into something bigger one day."

Leona shrugged. "Who knows? We sure can never guess what the Lord intends for us."

The idea that the Lord might have already put the perfect man in Effie's path while Mattie was still waiting and wondering when it was going to be her turn kind of pinched. Of course, she would never admit that. It was such a selfish thought!

But that didn't stop her from feeling a little melancholy about it.

As if reading her mind, Leona said sweetly, "Don't worry, Mattie. Your day will come. Who knows? Maybe Danny will make his move soon."

Mattie wrinkled her nose. "I doubt it."

"Patience is a virtue."

"You sound like my *mamm*."

Chuckling, Leona said, "Sorry, I guess I do. I hear what you're saying. It's just that I've learned that everything happens at the right time. Look how fast everything happened between me and Zack, I never expected to meet Zack while I was still engaged to Edmund! I really never expected to fall in love so fast, either."

Mattie supposed Leona had a point, though she privately thought it was fairly easy for Leona to sound comforting since she was just days away from getting hitched.

"I'm trying to remember that just because I would like to be in a relationship, doesn't mean that is what's best for me," Mattie said. "I need to remember to be happy with myself first." She breathed deeply as she picked up two squares of pale blue fabric and carefully pinned them together.

She was kind of proud of herself for sounding so grown up and mature. Inside, though, she knew she could easily dissolve into a childish temper tantrum. Sometimes she was so frustrated with herself and with her situation that she wanted to yell and jump up and down and ask the Lord why He'd made her the most unappealing girl in Walnut Creek.

Leona, of course, had no idea what she was thinking. So instead of looking concerned, she smiled. "I'm proud of you, Mattie. That is *gut* advice. You are someone all of us could learn from."

"Hardly."

"Well, you reminded me of something important. How about that?"

"I was reminded about something pretty important, too."

Leona gazed at her expectantly. "Oh? What was that?"

"I can't quilt as well as you."

"Oh, we already knew that," Leona teased. Pointing to the fabric lying around them, she said, "But that's not to say that you can't get better. That means we had better get busy and sew, sew, sew."

Mattie was just about to pick up her project again when the front door opened after a quick knock. Seconds later Zack entered the house with Danny at his side.

Immediately, Leona's contented expression turned into one of pure joy. "Zack, I didn't expect to see you until we went to the park tonight," she said as she crossed the room to her fiancé.

"I wasna planning to. I stopped by my parents' *haus*, fully expecting to help Effie with her exercises and maybe even do a load of laundry before I started looking for Serena, but my sister Violet had things well in hand." He grinned. "Then I remembered that Danny said he was getting off work a little early today. I stopped by his house and here we are."

Looking across the room, Mattie caught Danny's eye. For the first time since she'd arrived, he was smiling at her like she was special to him. When she smiled back and he didn't look away, her heart started beating a little faster.

This was what she'd been dreaming about when she made the decision to come back to Pinecraft.

At last it was happening!

Moments like this could be her future. She could spend afternoons with Leona, doing projects and gardening. Eventually they would be caring for their babies together, then one day running after their toddlers. They'd each have handsome men in their lives, men who just happened to also be best friends. They would have a lifetime of close friendships and togetherness.

It would be perfect. Wonderfully perfect.

Leona clasped her hands behind her back. "It's *gut* to see you both. Really *gut*. Don't you agree, Mattie?"

Mattie realized her hands were sweaty. "Oh, *jah*. It's *gut* to see you. Both. I mean, it's a nice surprise."

Zack looked like he was trying not to burst out laughing. "Leona, any chance you could make me a sandwich? I'm starving."

She turned toward the kitchen. "Of course. What would you like? I think we have ham and turkey."

"Hold up, Zack, wouldja?" Danny asked.

"What?"

"Would you mind if I didn't stay?"

And just like that, Mattie's euphoria plummeted. Only by sheer force of will did she manage to not close her eyes in disappointment.

"What do you need to do?" Zack asked.

Danny's gaze flickered toward Mattie. "I was hoping to spend some time with Mattie. Mattie, would you like to go for a walk with me?"

There went her heart again.

Oh, for heaven's sakes! How was she supposed to respond? If she sounded too eager she would come across as desperate. Too cool and he might regret finally making his move.

"Sure," she said at last. "I'd enjoy going for a walk with you, Danny."

"Going for a walk is a *wonderful-gut* idea," Leona stated. Probably a little too enthusiastically.

Danny stepped forward. "We could walk down to Olaf's and get a cone, if you'd like."

"That sounds like fun." She got to her feet, grabbed her coin purse, and glanced Leona's way. "I'll see you in a bit."

"Take your time," Zack said as he linked his fingers

in Leona's. "Like I said, I'm starving. Danny, Leona and I are going to Pinecraft Park around six."

"That sound okay with you, Mattie?" Danny asked. When she nodded, he said to Zack, "Mattie and me will meet you there."

"See you then," Leona said.

Mattie met Leona's gaze and smiled. "*Jah*. I'll see you then."

Chapter 5

It was amazing how a moment could surpass one's
most vivid expectations.

Here Mattie was, at last, walking by Danny
Brenneman's side on Beneva Road. He seemed relaxed
and casual, easygoing. Just as if they did this all the time.

Everything was perfect.

"I'm glad you stopped by, Danny," Mattie said, hoping
she didn't sound too excited.

He smiled down at her. "I am, too."

Already she felt warm inside. Finally! He was going
to tell her how much he'd liked being around her. "Oh?"

"For sure. I mean, you know how engaged couples are.
They can never have enough time alone."

Mattie felt her smile falter right in time with her confidence. She hadn't thought about that. She'd spent every
waking moment by Leona's side. Maybe she should have

taken more care to give them a few minutes of privacy every now and then.

"Do you think I am being a nuisance? Is that why you came to get me?"

"Oh, *nee*." Looking sheepish, he added, "I don't know why I just said what I did. I guess I'm not really used to courting and I was trying to act far more relaxed than I am."

He'd said *courting*. In their world, this wasn't a term used lightly. Two days ago, Mattie would have been practically swooning. But now she was simply confused. Did one walk constitute courting? She didn't believe so.

As they continued their walk toward Olaf's, passing a group of Amish from Pennsylvania dressed in pink dresses, white aprons, and heart-shaped *kapp*s, she knew she needed to speak her mind. As much as she'd been hoping for this moment, she wasn't eager to try and figure out what he meant. Maybe it was time for them both to speak frankly? "Danny, when I first got here, you hardly said more than hello. It really hurt my feelings since we've been exchanging letters for months now."

"We talked last night."

"We did," she allowed. "But we were all sitting around the Kaufmanns' kitchen table. Everyone was there. You had to know that I had thought you would have been more eager to spend some time with me."

"I didn't know what to say."

He sounded vaguely put upon. Mattie supposed she didn't blame him since she *was* forcing him to discuss their relationship—or lack of one. Quietly, she said, "Danny, I don't want to sound pushy, but I have been really trying to figure out what's going on."

"You just got here, Mattie. Plus, I've had to work and locate a crazy cat so Zack can have a happy wedding day."

Now she was embarrassed. "Sorry. I hadn't thought about all you've had to do. You see, I thought you didn't care for me any longer. I've been racking my brain, wondering what I did wrong."

Guiding her over to an empty parking lot, he shook his head. "You didn't do anything wrong."

A smart girl would smile and change the subject.

But she'd never been especially smart where relationships were concerned. Plus, well, they were on a time crunch. She was only going to be in Florida for another six days and one of those was Leona and Zack's wedding. "So, what are we doing now?" she asked lightly. "Are you courting me now? Or are you getting me out of Leona and Zack's hair so they can have some privacy?"

He sighed. "Do we have to label what we're doing?"

"Well, you did say 'courting.' That means something to me."

Danny visibly winced. "You're right. I did say that. But, um, I didn't mean that *we* were actually courting."

Yet again, he was speaking in riddles. And because of that, a bit of her fascination with him dimmed. Maybe they were meant to simply be friends. Or, at least, take things far more slowly.

"You know what, let's go get some ice cream," she said.

"And along the way, you can tell me how the search has been going for Serena."

A genuine smile crossed his features as they started walking again. "Zack told me that Mrs. Sadler gave him an earful when he stopped by her *haus* this morning before work."

"Oh, no. What happened?"

"It seems she barely said hello before launching into a tirade. Somehow it's now his fault that Serena is still missing."

Mattie winced. "She can be a mite difficult, hmm?"

"You don't know the half of it. I know she's worried about Serena, but she seems to expect Zack to search nonstop for a cat that doesn't seem to want to be found. If it was up to me, I'd tell Mrs. Sadler that she should put on her tennis shoes and start looking for that cat herself."

"I think I'd do the same thing," Mattie said around a giggle.

"*Jah?*" Danny's brown eyes warmed, as if he was thankful they had something in common. "Well, anyway, it isn't up to me. She dotes on Zack and he dotes on her, too. When I asked him what he did after she berated him, Zack said he simply stood there and listened."

"Zachary Kaufmann is a wonder."

Danny smiled. "Not quite. But maybe just where Mrs. Sadler is concerned."

As Mattie grinned, she relaxed for the first time since Danny had walked into that pretty sitting room. He was right; she needed to stop pushing and simply enjoy her time with him.

What would happen would happen.

JUST AS LEONA pulled out two packages of lunch meat for Zack, the kitchen door opened and her sisters and their husbands rushed in. After arriving that morning, Rosanna and Naomi had announced that they were going to go on a shopping run. Less than an hour later, they and their husbands were off and running.

As usual, Leona felt she was moving about two steps behind.

"Hi, girls," Naomi said as she set two sacks on the kitchen counter. "Help us unload these groceries."

"Zack will help you. I'm making him a sandwich."

"Sounds like you're spoiling him already," Rosanna teased as she, too, set down a sack.

"Making a sandwich ain't spoiling," Zack declared. "She's merely being nice."

"Zack, come out and help us get the rest of these groceries," Michael, Rosanna's husband, said as he walked out with David, Naomi's husband.

Leona smiled to herself as the five of them chattered back and forth while they brought in more sacks of groceries. This bantering about nothing was what she'd always hoped to have when she'd been engaged the first time. She'd wanted a partner who got along with her family. She'd wanted to have a man who could hold his own against her bossy sisters but who also was caring and sweet and full of life. Zack was all of those things.

After spreading a thin amount of mayonnaise on the

bread, she put the sandwich together, set it on a plate, and handed it to him after he set down the last sack on the counter. "Here you are," she said with a smile.

He leaned closer. "You really didn't mind making this for me, did ya?"

"Of course not, silly."

To her surprise, he leaned even closer, so close that his lips brushed her ear. "I love your family, but I canna wait to have you all to myself in a couple of days, Leona."

"Me too," she whispered right back, fully aware that a fierce blush was now staining her cheeks and neck.

"Enough of that, you two," Naomi said. "You're not married yet."

"Naomi, hush," Rosanna said. "Leave them alone. They look sweet."

Leona was sure she'd never been more embarrassed. "You two are the worst sisters ever."

But as she'd expected, her sisters merely shrugged off her comment. "Zack, because we like you, you may sit at the table and moon over Leona," Naomi stated with a wink.

"*Danke*," he said as he sat down. But when Leona was about to sit down beside him, Rosanna shook her head.

"Not you, Leona. Since we're all living here together in this rental house, you get to still be useful. Come help us unpack all these sacks."

"Anything else?" Leona asked sarcastically.

"Not at the moment. Though I expect you will have to let us tease you as much as possible."

"I'm glad things haven't changed too much," Leona

replied. But of course she was glad things hadn't really changed at all.

When she noticed that Zack was grinning broadly in her direction, she realized that things had, in fact, only gotten better.

Chapter 6

June 14

MATTIE WAS SO excited to be going the beach again, especially since she hadn't thought she was going to have time to get away.

The last couple of days had been busy. She'd helped Leona organize her new kitchen, look for Serena, and frost dozens upon dozens of cupcakes, since Leona and Zack had wanted cupcakes instead of a traditional wedding cake. And when they weren't doing any of those things, she and Leona been sewing.

Mattie had also spent an hour or two each day in Danny's company. She'd had fun with him, but she was starting to realize that they didn't have the spark between them that Leona and Zack did. At first she'd been disappointed but now she was realizing that one couldn't force things to happen that neither was ready for.

She supposed Danny felt the same way, though she wasn't sure. Yet again, he seemed to be confused about whether he liked her. Mattie wondered what would happen next when she got home. Did he like her well enough to book a bus trip to Walnut Creek? Would they start writing to each other again? Or were things simply going to fizzle out between them?

As they got off the SCAT at Siesta Key, Mattie breathed deeply. Already she could smell the ocean. "I'm so glad we're here," she said with a smile.

"Me too. It would be a shame if you came all the way to Florida and never saw the gulf," Danny said.

As they walked across the parking lot, they caught up on everything each of them had been doing in the past few days. Danny and a bunch of their friends had helped Zack move furniture into his new house. She'd stayed up late sewing the last of the placemats.

"Today feels like my first vacation day," Mattie admitted. "Though I came out here early to help Leona, I hadn't counted on being this busy."

"I hear you," Danny said as they walked down four concrete steps from the parking lot. At last, they were standing on the beach.

Mattie slipped off her flip-flops and wiggled her toes in the warm, sugary-soft sand. "This is *wunderbaar.*"

He laughed. "I agree."

After setting up their folding chairs and laying out their towels, Danny gestured toward the water. "Want to go for a walk along the shore?"

"Of course."

Though she'd put on a bathing suit under her dress, Mattie wasn't sure if she was going to be brave enough to actually pull off her dress and go swimming. Therefore, she simply tied a knot in the hem so the bottom of her dress secured at her knees.

That was good enough, she thought.

Danny had rolled up his pant legs to about mid calf. Mattie wondered if he, too, wasn't quite ready to be dressed only in a bathing suit when it was just the two of them.

As they started walking, Mattie did her best to keep the conversation bright and easy. She talked about her new love of crab cakes. She pointed out pretty shells. She admitted that she hoped she wouldn't have to make another placemat for at least a year. And she talked about the *kinner* in her classroom.

"I really love being a teacher," she admitted.

"I bet you're a good one. Walnut Creek is blessed to have you."

"Maybe one day you can visit me there," she said lightly.

"Maybe. I don't know."

Well, there was her answer. It seemed that they were destined to only be friends. "I see."

He darted a look her way, then sighed. "Mattie, I know you came to Florida expecting something from me, from us. And I want you to know that I do like you."

"But?"

"But, well, I'm not like Zack. I'm not ready to get in a serious relationship." After glancing at her again, he said, "I would still like to write you though . . . if you are willing to take things slowly. Really slowly."

"I'm not sure what *really slowly* means."

"It means I just got a new position in Zack's *daed*'s construction company. He made me a supervisor. I'm in charge of a crew now. I want to devote my energies to that." Before she could respond, he blurted, "I don't want to get married right away. Actually, I don't want to get married for a year or two. Maybe even three years."

"Three years is a long time."

"Is it too long for you?"

She taught school back in Walnut Creek. She loved her job and she loved working with *kinner*. She was also perfectly happy living at home and not having to be responsible for her own rent and bills and meals.

But did she want to continue things the way they were for years? She did not.

"So it's not that you don't like me. You do," she said, just to make sure she wasn't misunderstanding what he was saying. "You simply don't want to get involved with anyone anytime soon."

He smiled. "Exactly."

"Thank you for letting me know."

His smile faded. "Mattie, are you upset? I mean, sorry, I know you're upset. After all, I know you expected more from me after all those letters we exchanged."

"I'm not upset." She was disappointed but not devastated.

He wasn't the one.

And furthermore, having spent so much time with Leona, Mattie realized that their friendship was just as important as any future romantic relationship she would have. Leona was her best friend and always would be. She was blessed to have such a friend in her life, and it wasn't something to take for granted.

"Actually, I'm, ah, kind of glad that you don't want to be serious, Danny."

"Because you, too, don't want to rush into anything?" There was hope in his eyes.

Mattie couldn't say she blamed him. It would be the best of both worlds for him if she agreed to date him casually for years until he decided that he was willing to devote more energy to a romantic relationship.

But that wasn't what she wanted. While she hadn't been head over heels in love with Danny, she'd definitely had a crush on him. But that said, she had no desire to be a man's fallback plan. It would be pretty tough to resign herself to that kind of relationship.

No, the reason she was glad he wasn't serious was because she now knew he wasn't the man for her.

"I'm simply glad you were honest. I, uh, don't know when I'll be ready to marry. But I have a pretty good feeling I'll know when I'm ready because I'll want to be with the other person no matter what happens. I don't want to wait years hoping that one day you'll decide that you're finally ready to put me first."

"Oh." He shifted uncomfortably. A new glimmer entered his eyes. He looked a little troubled, like she'd given him something to think about that he hadn't planned on tackling. "So, um, what do you want to do now?"

Luckily, they just happened to be standing in front of a snack shack. "How about we get something to drink, then sit down and enjoy the beach?"

Slowly, he grinned. "That's it?"

She nodded. "There's no way I'm passing up the chance to sit at the beach."

"I'm glad we talked, Mattie. I'm, uh, glad you're not mad at me."

"I'm disappointed, but not mad. I'd like us to be friends, Danny."

"I can do friends."

She couldn't resist needling him. "You sure you have time for friendships?"

"Ouch. I guess I deserved that."

She grinned as they stepped into the short line at the snack shack. It seemed this vacation in Florida wasn't going to be full of romance after all. But that didn't mean she couldn't still have a good time.

LATER THAT NIGHT, Leona kept glancing at Mattie worriedly. "Are you sure you're going to be all right? I fear you're far more upset about what happened with Danny at the beach than you are letting on."

"I was disappointed, but like I told Danny, I'm not as upset as I thought I was going to be."

"I'm so glad. I'd feel so badly if you were crushed."

"I'm not crushed." After a pause, Mattie said, "You know, I was pretty upset with you when you broke off things with my *bruder*."

Leona's eyes flared with surprise for a moment. "I know you were upset. But, um, I thought you understood."

"I did," Mattie replied. "Edmund is my *bruder*, after all. I love him, but I also know his faults. He's a controlling, rather difficult sort. None of us can figure out how he got that way, if you want to know the truth."

Leona's voice was tentative. "He has always seemed like the odd man out in your house."

"Out of the five *kinner*, he's the one smack in the middle. Most folks say being a middle child means one is more flexible, but with him, I fear it's the opposite. He's like a giant tree trunk in the middle of everything. Growing up, the four of us would make plans on how to get around him."

Leona's lips twitched. "Especially you, Mattie. You've always been the most easygoing girl I know."

"I usually am. Anyway, what I'm getting at is though I said I understood why you fell in love with Zack so quickly, I didn't understand. Not really. I couldn't understand how years of courting could be erased with one single meeting."

Leona's eyes flashed with hurt. "It wasna one single meeting, Mattie. I wanted to stay true to my feelings for Edmund. I simply wasna able."

Mattie felt terrible. She was talking in circles so much that she was confusing Leona something awful and bringing up hurts that they'd both hoped would have been healed by now. "I'm not putting this well. What I'm trying to say is that I understand your feelings now."

"Because of what happened with Danny?"

"Partly. I wanted to be instantly, head over heels in love. I wanted to look at him and have us both know that we had each found the right person. Instead, I discovered that we were simply meant to be friends. And that I was all right with it."

Leona leaned into her, nudging her shoulder. "I'm sorry the romance you were hoping for didn't happen."

"I'm sorry, too. But it wasn't right of me to imagine that it could happen. The Lord doesn't work that way. Everything is in His time."

"*Jah.* We need to be like sheep instead of goats."

Mattie grinned. "Now that we've talked, want to go check on Mrs. Sadler?"

"You don't mind? I can go sit with her by myself if you'd like."

"*Nee*, silly. I have recently learned that it's far better to think of others than dwell on myself."

Leona smiled. "In that case, let's walk over and sit with Mrs. Sadler and hope and pray her cat shows up while we're there."

"I can do that," Mattie promised. In fact, that was one wish she sincerely hoped would come true.

Chapter 7

June 15

ALTHOUGH SHE STILL had too much to do, Leona was searching for Serena with Mattie yet again.

As they walked across a field, the short grass tickling their ankles, Leona said, "I hate to sound unkind, but I canna believe Zack talked me into doing this."

"You are doing it because you're a *wonderful-gut* fiancée," Mattie teased.

Because she didn't feel all that *wonderful-gut* at the moment, Leona didn't comment on that.

When they started walking along the back perimeter of Pinecraft Park, Mattie spoke again. "Do you think there really was a Serena sighting, or a false lead?"

"I couldn't begin to guess," Leona replied. "Zack told me that at least once a day someone knocks on his parents' house, claiming to have seen that cat."

"That's good news," Mattie said.

"Not really. As soon as they go outside to look, no one sees a thing."

"Maybe the signs Effie and her friends put up wasn't such a *gut* idea after all."

"Maybe not," Leona agreed. "So far they haven't helped much. Serena is still missing and poor Mrs. Sadler is sadder than ever. Still, it's not easy to give up hope."

"I would have to agree with you about that." Mattie sighed.

Leona looked at her curiously. "Are you talking about looking for Serena or something else?"

"Something else. Though I realize Danny isn't the man for me, I still am a little blue about it. I wanted things to work out with him so you and I could live near each other."

"For what it's worth, I wish it had," Leona said softly. She really did feel awful for Mattie.

As they left the park and started down the sidewalk along Bahia Vista, Mattie shook her head. "I can't believe how hopeful I was."

"Don't be so hard on yourself. Everyone has hopes and dreams."

"*Jah*, but they should be realistic ones. Just because Danny and I were friends didn't mean falling in love was around the corner. I expected too much."

"Mattie, I was engaged to your brother. And even when I was pretty sure that we weren't going to be a good match I kept my silence. I let my mother put deposits on the wedding wagon and make dresses for my sisters. Worse, I never made Edmund listen to me about my feelings."

"We know Edmund doesn't like to listen to other people."

"I still should have tried harder."

"In your defense, it turns out he was destined for someone else," Mattie pointed out. "Don't forget, he is seeing Tillie now."

Leona didn't want to spend another moment thinking about Edmund. "You know what? I've been looking in the branches of every tree we've passed but so far, I haven't seen a single cat."

"Me neither. I kind of feel like we've walked these same paths over and over and haven't had a bit of luck."

Lowering her voice so no one would overhear her, Leona said, "I'm beginning to fear that something happened to that cat. It's been *days* now. Poor thing."

"You read my mind," Mattie said. "Do you think Mrs. Sadler will ever accept that she needs to move on?"

Leona thought about that. "Honestly? *Nee.* She loves that cat. I feel sorry for her, but I think it's time we all faced the fact that the cat is gone for good."

"Zack needs to march over to Mrs. Sadler and tell her that. It would be a kindness."

Leona couldn't imagine Zack ever doing that. "It would be, but Zack doesn't know how to give up. As long as there's a chance he can fix things for Mrs. Sadler, he's going to do it. He calls it keeping the faith."

"I admire his determination, but I don't think I agree. I don't think it's a matter of having faith or not. It's more a matter of facing facts. That cat is gone."

Leona nodded. "I fear you are right but until then, we need to keep looking. Even though I've got my whole family here and a wedding to put on, Zack would be really disappointed if I didn't support him right now." Realizing that her voice was suddenly quivering, she sighed. All the commotion surrounding the wedding was beginning to take its toll. "Don't mind me. I'm just tired."

"You are getting married in two days, Le," Mattie said bluntly. "It's fairly obvious that you have other things to worry about besides a missing cat."

"This is true."

Looking around, Leona suddenly realized they were standing in a field behind Pinecraft Elementary. Nearby was a gas station and convenience store. And just to the side of that was a worn-looking picnic table. It looked like the perfect place to relax and catch their breath. "Would you mind if we sat down for a minute?"

"Not at all. I think it is definitely time to take a break."

Once they reached the picnic table, Leona sat down and sighed. "I'm sorry, Mattie. This has been a stressful day. My sisters are here, and my mother woke me up with a dozen questions about the food, and Zack doesn't seem to want to talk about the reception."

"I betcha every bride has one or two stressful moments before her wedding day."

"I bet you are right. It would be impossible not to feel stressed about such a big event."

"I hope I'm wrong." Mattie winked. "I hope my wedding day—if it ever happens—will be relaxed and easy."

Leona chuckled. "I don't. I want things to be just as crazy for you."

"If it ever happens."

"It will happen." She was just about to reassure Mattie

yet again that everything would turn out for her when she heard a scratching noise. "What was that?"

Mattie tilted her head. "What's what?"

"That noise. Didn't you hear it?"

"*Nee.*"

"Listen." When she heard the scratching again, she leapt to her feet. "That was it! It's over this way."

"Leona, I still don't hear a thing."

"Follow me, then." She kept walking, hoping her ears weren't deceiving her. Mattie, being the friend she was, kept by her side, her gaze focused steadily on the ground.

After five minutes, Leona felt foolish. "I guess it was just a branch rustling in the wind."

"It's not windy, Le."

"You know what I mean. It's probably nothing, just an overactive—"

Meow!

Hope burst in Leona's chest before she firmly tamped it down. Surely after all the searching and praying and days spent in a futile effort to calm Mrs. Sadler, it couldn't be this easy?

Meow. Immediately, they veered left.

After a few more cries, they came upon a ravine and spied a gray cat curled in a tight ball. She looked up at them pitifully. "Oh, Serena!" Leona cried.

Abruptly, Mattie stopped and grabbed her arm. "Leona, I think we have just solved the mystery."

After emitting another pitiful meow, the cat whimpered when Leona dropped to her knees beside her.

And then Leona saw what had kept Serena away for so

long. Snuggled next to her were four tiny gray and black kittens. Their eyes were closed and their tiny paws were pink. It was the sweetest sight Leona had ever seen.

"Oh my goodness! Serena, look at you!" she said.

Immediately, Mattie knelt by her side. "Careful, Leona," she began as she leaned close, then gasped. "Kittens!"

Leona felt her eyes tear up. Serena had made a nest in the field and had her kittens, but had been unable to leave them to get food or water. Thank goodness Zack had wanted them to keep looking for her. Thank goodness she and Mattie had been right here to find her!

Gently, she reached out and petted the cat. When Serena closed her eyes and leaned toward Leona's hand, Leona looked at Mattie. Mattie, too, was crying.

"I'm so glad we found her," Mattie whispered. "God is so good."

"He is, indeed. We better get her and the kittens to Mrs. Sadler."

"Since Serena knows you, you take her. I'll carry the kittens in my apron," Mattie said.

Now that they had a plan, Leona lifted Serena into her arms hesitantly. She was afraid Serena might protest being separated from her kittens, but instead of fighting, the little cat snuggled close. "Oh, Serena, you poor dear," she murmured. As she got to her feet, she noticed that she was damp and bedraggled.

Then Serena meowed at Mattie.

"Don't worry, silly girl," Mattie said as she carefully picked up all four kittens and gathered them in the apron she'd taken off. "I've got your babies just fine."

"Poor Serena," Leona murmured. "I bet she's so tired. Let's go show them to Zack, then he can be in charge of getting Serena and her sweet kittens home."

Holding the precious cargo close to her heart, Mattie smiled. "You and Serena lead, and the kittens I will follow. I can't wait to see everyone's faces when they see what we found."

"Me, neither," Leona said as they started back across the field. "Everyone is going to be so happy."

"This is simply the best day, ever," Mattie proclaimed.

Though Leona smiled in agreement, she couldn't help but hope that her upcoming wedding day would be even better.

Chapter 8

MATTIE WAS BEGINNING to think she'd taken her family's barn cats at home for granted. For most of her life, she assumed they were happy enough roaming around the barn and fields hunting for mice. She'd never given them a lot of thought. Actually, she only took notice of them when they were lying in the sun or needed something. But after witnessing the reunion of Serena and Mrs. Sadler, she was starting to think that those cats probably could have used a bit more attention.

Though she suspected that a person would have to be made of clay to not be genuinely affected by Winnie Sadler's reaction to seeing Serena and her brood of adorable kittens.

"You brought her back!" she exclaimed when Zack handed over a very tired and disgruntled-looking Serena. "*Danke*, Zack."

"You should be thanking Leona and Mattie. They are the ones who found her."

"Thank you, girls," she said. "After she kissed the top of the cat's head, tears entered her eyes. "Oh, just look at her. Serena is beautiful."

"*Jah*, she looks mighty pretty, Mrs. Sadler," Zack murmured. "And she brought you a few presents, too."

Mrs. Sadler looked at him in confusion. "What?"

"Here," Leona said as she held up a plastic laundry hamper. It was lined with an old soft sheet and held Serena's tiny family. Before coming to Mrs. Sadler's house, Mattie, Leona, Zack, and Danny had fed Serena and attempted to clean both the cat and her kittens with some warm washcloths. Now the kittens looked a little fluffier and somehow even cuter.

Immediately Mrs. Sadler got to her feet and peered in the hamper. Then she gasped. "My word!"

Zack chuckled as Leona set the hamper on the porch. "It seems Serena had a beau of her own and now she has four kittens."

"They are precious, aren't they?" Mrs. Sadler asked as Serena meowed, then hopped into the hamper and curled around the kittens.

They all watched as Serena fussed with each of her babies while they nursed, licking their fur and generally acting like the devoted mother she was.

"Leona, you and Mattie are simply angels!"

"I wouldn't say that, Mrs. Sadler," Leona said.

"I certainly would." Her voice softened. "Girls, I don't know if you'll ever understand what having Serena back safe means to me. All I can say is that you've made me so very happy." After wiping away a stray tear, she continued. "And these kittens, well, they are simply tiny miracles."

"They are, indeed," Leona said. "I love them already."

"I think that means you're going to have a kitten soon, Zack," Danny whispered.

"*Jah.* I know." Though Zack attempted to look put-upon, Mattie couldn't resist giggling.

After returning to her chair on the porch, Mrs. Sadler gazed at each of them. "Thank you all again," she said in a quivering voice. "I fear I must admit that I'd begun to lose hope. *Danke* for reminding me how important it is to keep my faith."

"We only tried to help," Leona said gently as she patted the older lady's arm. "It just happened to be me and Mattie who heard Serena crying in that ditch. It could have been any of us."

"But it was you, dear. And for that, I will always be grateful. To both of you."

"I'm simply glad she and her kittens were found," Mattie mumbled.

"You girls kept your faith. I have much to learn from you both."

"You don't have anything to learn from us," Mattie blurted. "I have a lot to learn from you about how to care for a pet."

As Mrs. Sadler smiled, Serena fussed with her kittens. After another minute or two, it became obvious that she was ready to take a nap now that she and her babies were safe and warm.

After giving a rather exaggerated yawn, Zack said,

"We ought to be going now. I think Serena needs her rest."

Winnie nodded. "That might be a mighty *gut* idea. I'm rather tired now, too."

After yet another round of thanks, Mattie, Leona, Danny, and Zack left Mrs. Sadler's house. They all kept their silence for a good half block, then, one by one, each started laughing.

"Kittens!" Danny said. "Who would have thought?"

"Not me," said Mattie.

"Me neither," Zack said. "I just wanted to find that cat." Looking at his fiancée fondly, he said, "And I can't believe Mrs. Sadler gave you all the credit."

"Well, me and Mattie did find her."

"It's hardly fair," Danny said around a grin. "Zack and I did all the work."

"It *is* because of you both that we were even looking," Mattie admitted.

"Well, it doesn't matter who gets the credit, as long as Mrs. Sadler has her cat back," Zack said. "And of course, her four kittens."

As they continued on their way, Danny quipped, "*Nee*, what matters is that the cat now looks determined to stay home. I hope she stays put with her kittens for a few weeks."

"At the very least, until Leona and I get married," Zack said.

"*Jah*," she said sweetly. "I will hope and pray that Serena the cat stays home at least for the next couple of days. Though it's a selfish hope, I think the good Lord will understand."

When Leona giggled again and leaned closer to her fiancé, Mattie slowed a bit so Leona could enjoy some quiet time with Zack. Soon, she noticed that Danny was keeping pace next to her.

She felt herself blush when he glanced her way.

"Is me walking with you going to bother you, Mattie?"

"*Nee*. I mean, as long as it doesn't bother you."

"Are you upset with me? About what I said?"

"I thought I would be," she said lightly. "I mean, I have to tell you that I was fairly sure we were going to fall in love and all . . . but I ended up realizing that you were right. I think we are more suited to be friends."

Pure relief entered his expression. "I can't tell you how happy I am to hear you say that."

"You were that worried about my feelings for you?"

"*Nee*. I was that worried that we were going to lose our friendship."

His honest words made her heart warm. "You mean that, don't you?"

"*Jah*. Girlfriends might come and go, but I've learned that true friendships are far harder to acquire. I feel that we've become true friends. I didn't want to lose that."

Mattie hadn't wanted to lose that, either. And, as she thought about her experiences with Leona today, accidentally finding Serena, laughing and smiling at each other, knowing that so much could be said without a single word being uttered, Mattie realized that Danny was right.

Crushes and infatuation could come and go. But true friendship? That was something to be cherished.

Chapter 9

June 17

LEONA'S WEDDING DAY dawned clear and bright, like a perfect photo straight out of a magazine. She'd greeted the rising sun with a happy smile, feeling so blessed to be celebrating her wedding in such a beautiful place.

However, by the time the clock in the Kaufmanns' kitchen chimed six times, clouds had come in. By half past six that morning, the sky had turned distinctly overcast, bringing with it a suffocating humidity.

Everyone present, from thirteen-year-old Effie to Zack's older brother Karl to Leona's father Henry had something to say about it.

By six forty-five, Leona, her mother, Mattie, and Zach's mother Ginny were staring up into the sky with matching frowns.

"Oh, dear. I am sorry, Leona, but I fear that it's going to rain," Mamm said.

Mattie nodded. "It sure does look that way."

Leona sighed. Though it wasn't the end of the world, it was disappointing. Karl, Zach, and their *daed* had spent most of the previous day erecting the white tent in the Kaufmanns' backyard. Now she was going to have to worry about everyone dodging raindrops as they went to and from the house.

"Maybe the rain will pass," Mattie said with a trace of a smile. After a sip of coffee, she said, "Sometimes those clouds don't mean a thing."

Still staring at the sky, Leona frowned. "I think these clouds mean rain. And by the time it passes, my wedding will be over. This is really too bad."

Ginny squeezed her shoulder, "Don't worry, Leona. I'm gonna make this right."

Mattie wrinkled her nose. "How are you going to do that?"

Ginny smiled. "We're moving the wedding and reception into the house." Raising her voice, she said, "*Kinner*, come over here and listen. You too, Rosanna and Naomi."

Leona hid a smile as even her older sisters and their husbands followed directions.

"Here's what we're going to do . . ." Ginny began. Then, with lightning speed, she started calling out names and telling them where to put all the living room furniture.

In seconds, the room was going to dissolve into utter chaos, and all just hours before Leona spoke vows she intended to keep for a lifetime.

"Mamm!" Leona hissed. "Say something."

Lifting her chin a bit, her mother blurted, "Do you think moving the wedding inside is necessary, Ginny? After all, no one ever melted from a little rain."

Before Leona could give her mother a relieved smile,

Zack's *mamm* shook her head. "Oh, we're going to get a whole lot more than just a few raindrops, Edie. It's going to storm."

"How do you know?" Mattie asked.

"I just do."

After receiving a not-so-subtle nudge in the ribs from her *mamm*, Leona's *daed* walked closer to the open door and peeked up at the sky. "Lucky for us, we have a sturdy tent. We'll be fine."

"*Nee*, we won't," Ginny stated. "We need to move everything now."

Leona gaped. "But—"

"Leona, dear," Frank, Zach's dad, said, "If Zack was here, he'd tell you the same thing I'm going to. We need to listen to Ginny."

"We kinda do," Effie said around a groan.

Mattie set down her coffee cup and crossed her arms over her chest. "Because?"

"Our mother is a regular weather barometer," Violet said. "She always can predict what the weather is going to be like."

"It's kind of a shame that we live in Florida," Karl added with a grin. "The weather service could really use her up north."

"But, ah, don't you think it's too late to rearrange everything? After all, we already have all the flowers set up," Leona's mother fretted. "And the area for the buffet."

"Oh, we'll make room for the flowers. And we'll set up the buffet in the kitchen," Ginny said. "Don't you worry about a thing, Edie."

Her mother's expression turned pained. "But—"

As much as she appreciated her parents' efforts to change Mrs. Kaufmann's mind, it was obvious it was a lost cause. Therefore, it was time to step in. "*Danke*, but it's all right, Mamm. I just want to get married to Zack." When her *mamm* still looked determined to argue her point, Leona reached for Mattie's hand and squeezed.

And, just like the stellar maid of honor she was, Mattie came to the rescue. She took a deep breath, seemed to summon up her teacher voice, and said, "Ginny, let's get started. Just tell me what to do and I'll do it."

"*Jah*, let's get busy," Rosanna said. "People will be arriving before we know it."

The mention of time seemed to spur everyone on like nothing else. As Ginny called out orders for everyone to move furniture and flowers, Leona and her mother reorganized the kitchen for the buffet. Leona thought they all resembled a colony of ants, the way everyone worked so well together.

Thirty minutes later, the rain began to fall.

Mattie escorted Leona upstairs so they could change into their matching blue dresses, white aprons, and black *kapps*, and thirty minutes after that, the rest of their friends and family arrived. Leona was sitting next to Mattie and her sisters as she stared at Zachary, who was sitting across the aisle next to Danny and Karl.

Three hours later, after the last preacher said his final prayer, they were married.

And still it poured.

Zack walked Leona to the back of his living room,

where their family had set up a long table with the blue patchwork table runner that Leona had made and a long line of Mattie's blue placemats on either side.

As he helped her sit down, he leaned in close. "Are you upset about the rain?"

Leona looked up at him and shook her head. "*Nee*."

"Sure?"

"Positive. Though I would have liked more space for everyone, I don't mind it being inside as long as everyone else is happy."

He brushed his lips against her cheek. "You are the one who is supposed to be happy, Le. This is your day."

"*Nee*, it's *our* day, and I couldn't be happier, Zack. I'm here with you. It's a perfect day."

His dimples appeared. "I agree, Mrs. Kaufmann. It's a *wonderful-gut* day."

And later, as everyone ate cupcakes and laughed and enjoyed themselves, Leona shared a smile with Mattie.

It seemed that even though all their wishes hadn't come true, they had remembered what was most important:

The beauty in simple vows, enduring friendship, family, security, and love.

Chapter 10

June 18

THE LUMP IN Mattie's throat threatened to choke her as the bus pulled out of the parking lot behind Village Pizza and headed down Bahia Vista toward the highway.

Mattie couldn't believe the visit she'd been anticipating for so long was already over. She was going back to Ohio with nothing more to look forward to but her regular life back in Walnut Creek. Of course, as soon as she thought such a thing, she felt guilty. She should be counting her blessings, not dwelling on things that couldn't be.

The Lord was in charge, for sure and for certain. And that meant she needed to realize that her future was back in Ohio, not Florida. He'd shown her time and again that this was His wish.

And He was right. She had a wonderful life in Walnut Creek. Her family was there, as were all her friends. And her job. She loved being a teacher. What's more, she was even good at it. Though some people might disagree, teaching school wasn't all that easy. She was blessed to excel at something that touched so many lives.

So, yes, that was a blessing.

Furthermore, there were many eligible men in her church district, too. And though she'd never been especially attracted to any of them, that could change. Why, maybe one day one of the men she'd known since childhood would feel like the right man for her. That very thing had happened to her eldest sister; Marjorie had married a man she'd known for all her life: the eldest son of the farmer next door.

What Mattie needed to remember was that Marjorie had never given up or lost faith that she would have everything she always wanted. She'd been steadfast in her belief that everything would happen when the Lord intended it to. Actually, Mattie thought Marjorie would have been mighty upset if anyone had ever questioned God's timing.

Why couldn't she be more like that? Was her faith really that immature?

She hoped not. She made a point right then and there to become more positive, to only think about things she was thankful for instead of the things she wished would happen.

If she could do that, she would surely be happier.

The bus drove along the busy streets, passing bicyclists and tourists, scooter-riding teenagers and Englischer residents, too. Yes, it was a new day. Everyone had gotten up and was moving forward. And that was exactly what Mattie should do.

After all, it had been a successful trip. She and Leona had sewed all her placemats and napkins and tablecloths, too. Everything had turned out beautifully and looked especially pretty in the tent erected in the Kaufmanns' backyard—well, until the rain had come and they'd moved everything into the house. Then, of course, there was the whole reason for Mattie's visit. She'd gotten to sit by Leona's side and witness her best friend's happiness. Leona had looked so happy and her voice had been sure and clear when she'd said her vows.

Mattie was sure that everyone present had felt the same thing she did—that Leona and Zack were meant to be together.

And, after ten days of searching and cajoling, Serena and her kittens had been found. Now the cat seemed content and happy to be home. The kittens were moving around more and even seemed to have gotten a little bigger in just the few days since their rescue. They were adorable and precious. Mrs. Sadler had even joked about how hard it was going to be to part with them.

That had been a wonderfully happy ending to be sure.

So, actually, the only disappointing part of the trip had been everything that had happened with Danny. And even she could admit that was partly her fault. Danny had never acted as if she was everything to him. He'd never acted as if they had a future or as if he was intending to court her soon.

No, that dream had been all hers.

Around her, people began to settle. Some opened puzzle books and novels. A pair of teenage boys pulled out some Uno cards. Another woman opened up a tote bag and pulled out a skein of yellow yarn and a crochet hook.

Most everyone else was talking quietly.

Life had moved on and she needed to do that, too. With a sigh, she opened her own tote bag and pulled out a book she'd borrowed from Leona. If she couldn't have her own romance, she might as well get lost in a fictitious one.

"Any chance you have an extra pen in there?"

Startled, she looked to her right. The dark-haired man across the aisle was staring back at her intently. "Pardon me?"

He held up a book of word searches. "I brought this book but of course forgot to grab a pen." He had dark green eyes.

"Oh. Sure." She opened her bag and started digging around again. "I know I have one in here someplace."

He shifted, enabling him to face her better. Allowing her to see that he was broad-shouldered and lanky. And that his bare forearms were very tan. "Take your time. We're going to be here for another twenty hours."

"Don't remind me. It always feels longer going home."

He studied her. "Have you made this trip a lot?"

"Only one other time. You?"

"This was my first time."

"Oh, did you like Pinecraft? What did you do?"

As if he was aware of several people glaring at them because they were talking a little too loudly, he said, "Do you mind if I come sit beside you for a while? It's easier to talk that way instead of across the aisle."

"I don't mind." She scooted to the empty seat next to her and watched as he took the seat she'd just vacated.

"*Danke*," he murmured. Leaning closer, he murmured, "I think we were starting to annoy everyone around us."

He smelled good. Like fresh soap and shampoo. She swallowed. "Maybe so." She dug in her bag again and then at last pulled out a pen. "Here you go."

He took it from her. "Thanks. Want to help me?"

"Sure." When he opened the book to the first page, she tried to concentrate on the puzzle, she really did, but all she seemed to notice was that his jaw was square and he was far bigger than she. Why, she guessed he was at least six feet. And his hands . . . they looked strong and capable.

Afraid of the direction of her thoughts, she cleared her throat. "Did you come down here by yourself?"

"*Nee.* I met some friends of mine. A couple of my buddies are getting married in November. We decided to come down for a week before things got busy on our farms."

He was a farmer. "Where do they live?"

"In Charm, same as I do." Looking a little embarrassed, he added, "I got the dates mixed up when I booked the bus ticket so I'm leaving a day earlier."

She couldn't resist smiling. "That sounds like something I would do."

Those green eyes of his sharpened. "Really?"

She had to be honest. "Well, not really. I'm a teacher, so I'm pretty good at making plans."

He grinned. "I'm a farmer, so I'm pretty used to realizing that most things are out of my control. It seems even bus tickets are."

She felt a little flutter as she smiled back at him. Her body's response took her by surprise. Had this ever happened with Danny? At the moment, for some reason, she couldn't remember.

"What about you?" he asked. "Are you traveling alone?"

"*Jah*. My best friend, Leona, just got married. I came down to Pinecraft to be here for the wedding. Her family is going to stay longer."

"So, you're from the North, too?"

"I am."

"Where do you live?"

"Walnut Creek."

"Ain't that something? Here we are on a bus in Florida and it turns out that we live close to each other."

"It is something. I'm Mattie. Mattie Miller."

"I'm Ben Borntrager. It's nice to meet you."

She smiled softly as she realized she felt the same exact way. "It's nice to meet you, too, Ben."

She wasn't sure what was going to happen next, but she was pretty sure it would be something pretty wonderful.

And this time, she was simply going to hold on and let things happen the way the Lord intended them to. One day at a time.

It seemed her trip to Pinecraft was a success after all, and her wish to find a partner in life just might have come true.

All she'd had to do was believe. Believe, dream, hope . . . and have faith.

Author's Note

Dear Reader,

One of my favorite things about writing this series was working with my editor and an artist on the map of Pinecraft that is in each book of the series. As you might imagine, designing the map took quite a bit of the artist's time, so my job was to provide as many "made-up" places and characters as I could while writing the first book in the series, The Promise of Palm Grove.

Though some writers prepare pages of notes before writing the first word, I'm afraid I'm not like that. It's only while writing that characters and places come alive for me. That's great . . . except when one is asked to list places that might be in the third or fourth book in a series!

However, I gave it my best effort. I knew I wanted a beagle in the book, a coffee shop, and the Orange Blossom Inn. And, as an afterthought, I added Serena the cat. Serena is the reason Zack and Leona meet in

The Promise of Palm Grove *so I thought she would be a good character for the artist to add. Then, I kind of forgot about her . . . until I decided to write this novella.*

When I began to plot A Wish on Gardenia Street, *I knew I wanted two characters to shine: Mattie and Serena! Mattie, because this was her story, and Serena, because I was starting to feel kind of sorry for that little cat. Here she had a lovely picture on the map but was hardly ever mentioned. I have to admit that I'm very fond of how her story turned out.*

I hope you enjoyed A Wish on Gardenia Street, *too. Thank you for visiting Pinecraft with me!*

Blessings,

Shelley

Your vacation in Pinecraft doesn't end here!
Don't miss the first two books
in Shelley Shepard Gray's
Amish Brides of Pinecraft series,

THE PROMISE OF PALM GROVE

And

THE PROPOSAL AT SIESTA KEY

Available now from Avon Inspire
wherever books are sold.

And keep reading for sneak peeks from

A WEDDING AT THE
ORANGE BLOSSOM INN

And

A CHRISTMAS BRIDE IN PINECRAFT

Coming Fall 2015

An Excerpt from

A WEDDING AT THE
ORANGE BLOSSOM INN

In New York Times *best-selling author
Shelley Shepard Gray's third book in her Amish Brides of
Pinecraft series, a wedding brings together two young wid-
owed parents . . . and gives them a second chance at love.*

WHEN THEY'D GOTTEN out to the sidewalk, Jay had
pulled out a sheet of paper listing a couple of restaurants
within easy walking distance but outside the heart of
Pinecraft. They had ended up having Italian food. Emma
had jumped at the chance to take the SCAT and dine
someplace where it was unlikely that they'd see anyone
she knew.

And they hadn't.

Therefore, instead of feeling like she and Jay were

being observed, they were able to simply enjoy each other's company. Instead of wondering what the gossipmongers would say or rush to tell her parents, she'd focused on herself and her feelings and slowly let down her guard.

And they'd talked. Oh, how they'd talked! About childhoods and school while eating Caesar salads, about hobbies and what they'd done during their *rumspringa*s, while eating far too much of the chef's delicious baked ziti. They'd talked about favorite foods and foods they hated as they split a decadent plate of cheesecake with fresh strawberry sauce.

And as each course came and went, Emma found herself opening up even more. She laughed a little more easily, shared more personal stories. And she listened to Jay a little more closely. She soaked in every sweet look and kind gesture.

Now, after taking the SCAT bus back to Pinecraft, Jay was walking her home down Kaufmann Avenue. She felt flirty and giddy. Found herself smiling whenever he glanced her way . . . and discovered she couldn't seem to stop gazing at him. None of this felt especially mature or anything like the behavior a mother of three should be exhibiting! Actually, she felt just like one of the teenagers she saw off in the distance—light and carefree.

"You've gotten quiet all the sudden," Jay said. "Did I talk your ear off?"

"Not at all. I guess I was simply thinking about what a nice time I had with you tonight."

"I enjoyed myself, too." He looked like he was tempted to add something more, but he said nothing else. "You are easy to talk to. I, um, shared more with you tonight than I have with anyone in the last year."

"I feel the same way. I was actually hoping you didn't think I was talking *your* ear off," Emma admitted, "or I'd revealed too much about myself." Maybe she'd told him too many stories about being a single mother.

"I liked hearing all of it from you."

"It's been a long time since anyone wanted to know so much about me."

He smiled. "That's the price of parenthood, I guess. It's never about us anymore. It's about the *kinner*."

"It's always about the *kinner*," she agreed. "And that is as it should be. Though sometimes . . ."

"Sometimes it is nice to remember that there is more to us than just being someone's father or mother."

"Exactly." She was glad he understood.

But as she looked around, she realized they were just steps from her house. After all that worrying and fretting she'd done, her date was finished and she felt slightly empty. "I canna believe it's over," she murmured.

"What is?"

"Our date."

He held out a hand to help her up the steps. She liked the way it felt in hers, liked the way he seemed to enjoy her touch as much as she enjoyed his. "I'm sorry it's over, too. But maybe we'll do it again sometime soon?"

"Are you asking me out again?" She really hoped he thought she was merely teasing.

"*Jah*, though it seems I'm doing a poor job of it. Will you go out with me again?"

"Yes."

"What about your parents? Are you willing to go up against them again?"

Until that moment, she hadn't been sure if she was strong enough. But now she knew she wasn't going to let anything stop her from having another night like this. "I'm willing. They are going to have to find a way to accept my decision." Just as she was going to have to find a way to convince them of it.

He smiled as they walked up the steps, her hand still securely clasped in his. When they reached her front door, he held out his hand for her keys. She handed them to him and stood quietly while he unlocked the door. Then she felt a moment of panic. Did she invite him in? Did he expect to kiss her good night? Would he be shocked if she actually *did* kiss him good night?

His expression was warm as he watched her. "It's okay, Emma. All I'm going to do is say good night to you right here."

"You knew what I was thinking?" She wasn't sure if she was mortified or extremely relieved.

He nodded. "As clearly as if you were saying it out loud." Folding his arms over his chest, he grinned. "I know what you were thinking because I'm pretty sure I was thinking the same thing."

"Which was?"

"That I don't want to leave you yet. I would love for you to invite me in, but I'm afraid every one of your neighbors is watching quietly from their windows. I don't want to do that to you."

Feeling a little sheepish, she said, "I fear you are right. My neighbors are wonderful, but they're not exactly afraid to be nosy, either."

"I don't want tonight to end because I like being with you. But the only remedy I can think of for easing our unhappiness is to make plans to see each other again. Will you go out with me again soon?"

"*Jah*," she answered. She didn't know how she was going to manage it but she would make it happen.

"I'll see you soon, then." Reaching out, he ran a finger along her cheekbone. "If we weren't likely being observed, I'd try to kiss you good night. Would you let me?"

There it was. That gentle flirting again. It made her smile . . . and made her want to flirt a little bit back. "Maybe."

"Maybe?"

"If I told you all my secrets you'd have no reason to want to see me again."

"You would be wrong about that, Emma. I would want to see you soon, even if I knew every one. *Gut naught.*"

"*Gut naught*, Jay. *Danke.*"

With one last lingering smile, he turned and walked away.

And when she went inside, she could practically hear the pounding of her heart.

An Excerpt from

A CHRISTMAS BRIDE IN PINECRAFT

Christmas has come to Pinecraft in best-selling author Shelley Shepard Gray's final Amish Brides of Pinecraft novel—an uplifting story that proves anything is possible when you follow your heart.

BEVERLY LOOKED AT Eric in surprise when he strode into the kitchen half an hour later. She'd pulled everything out of one of the cabinets and had a bottle of spray cleaner in her hands.

"Beverly, what are you doing? I told you we needed to talk."

"We can talk while I clean the cabinets."

"You suddenly decided you needed to clean them?"

"I'm, uh, taking stock, too."

"Bev."

She kept her eyes focused on something just to his left. "You know I've been going through everything since the robbery."

"Nobody stole anything from the cabinets. We both know that. Besides, you organized it the other day. I stood here and watched you."

Those green eyes of hers that he loved so much filled with distress. "I need to keep busy, Eric."

His heart softened as he heard the distress in her voice, too. He walked to her side and took the bottle of cleaner out of her hand. Then kept his hands on hers and gently squeezed. "I can appreciate that, but you aren't behaving rationally. I'm worried about you, Bev."

"Thank you for that, but there is no need to worry. I am fine."

"You are not fine at all. You are working yourself into a dither, and I am concerned."

She pulled her hands from his and crossed them over her chest. "I don't get into *dithers*, Eric. I have merely been cooking and cleaning and getting the inn organized."

"That's *all* you've been doing."

"We had a robbery. Strangers went through the whole inn. They stole a television, remember?"

"I bought a new one."

"Things are a mess."

"No, things *were* a mess. Now everything is bright and shiny. It looks as pretty as I've ever seen it."

She looked up at him in wonder. Her wide-set eyes appeared even greener than usual, thanks to the forest green dress she was wearing. And though her brown hair was pinned up, more than a couple of strands had fallen around her face, making her appear younger. And, to his surprise, even prettier. Bemused, he found himself leaning against the doorjamb that led to the back patio, content to simply admire her—which wasn't good, seeing as how it was absolutely *not* why he'd wanted to talk to her.

"Eric? You are staring." She fidgeted, pushing a lock of hair back behind her ear and smoothing her dress.

"I know." Unable to keep a straight face, he grinned.

"Why are you staring at me? And smiling? What's wrong?"

"Not a single thing. I'm simply taken with you."

"Surely not. Have you never seen a woman organize a kitchen before?"

He honestly couldn't say that he had. He'd never dated a woman seriously enough to be around her when she was simply doing chores at home. But he couldn't say that. "Not one who wore a pretty green dress while she did it."

Now she was looking flustered. Which was good. Now, at least, they were on even ground.

She brushed back another strand of hair. Honestly, every strand looked in serious danger of escaping from its pins and falling around her shoulders.

"Let's go play hooky for a little while."

"I'm not going to the beach, Eric."

"I wasn't thinking about Siesta Key. I was thinking that we should go shopping."

"I can't go shopping for groceries until I finish this inventory."

"Not for food." Suddenly the perfect idea came to him. "Let's go get a Christmas tree."

"A what?" Her eyes were wide and a look of true dismay filled her expression.

He chuckled. "Beverly, you do know what a Christmas tree is, right? One of those green things you put lights on? Decorate with bright, shiny ornaments?"

"There's no need to use that tone. Of course I know what a Christmas tree is. It's just that the Amish don't have Christmas trees." Standing up a bit primly, she said, "The Amish don't believe in the need for all of those commercial entrapments to celebrate Jesus's birthday."

She looked so earnest it took everything he had to keep from smiling. "I know that."

"If you know that, then you must also know that I do not want a Christmas tree in the inn."

It was time to pull out the big guns. "Did you forget that this is technically my inn?"

"*Nee.* Of course I didn't forget that."

Taking care to keep his tone light, he added, "And, I don't know if you've noticed, but I'm not Amish."

"I know you aren't."

"And, last time I checked, you weren't, either."

After staring at him a moment longer, Beverly turned to the refrigerator, pulled out a pitcher of cold water, poured herself a tall glass, and drank half of it. "Eric, I may not be Amish anymore, but that don't mean I want to start adopting all kinds of fancy English traditions."

Though Eric had wanted a Christmas tree anyway, he'd suggested it mainly as something they could do to get her mind off the robbery. But now he was starting to think that they needed one really just to shake things up a bit.

Actually, a green tree in the window would look really pretty. Festive.

"I'm not talking about purchasing an inflatable Santa and sticking him on your lawn, Bev," he said gently. "Instead, I think we should head to the empty lot next to the hardware store and buy us a six- or seven-foot Christmas tree. A real one, so the whole room will smell like Christmas."

"Like evergreens," she mused. "Heavenly."

"It would be perfect." If he hadn't seen the fresh wave of longing in her eyes, he would have thought he'd imagined it. He pressed a bit further. "We don't even have to put any ornaments on it if you don't want."

Ironically, she looked a bit peeved. "Eric, we can't have a plain, bare tree simply sitting around. What would people say?"

It was becoming difficult to keep a straight face. "How about we put lights on it? Just a bunch of white lights?"

"White lights would look pretty."

"Christmassy, yet plain."

"The Amish don't use electricity. So not too Plain."

He started laughing. "You are so literal sometimes, Beverly Overholt. Honestly, you crack me up. I meant that we won't have a tree with all kinds of ornaments and stuffed birds hanging from the branches."

"Absolutely not. We have birds outside."

She sounded so prim and proper, he was tempted to

remind her that there were trees outside, too, but he was pretty sure that would work against his plan. "So what do you say? Will you go get a Christmas tree with me?"

She bit her lip, glanced at her coffee cup, then seemed to have made her decision. "*Jah*."

"Thank you. I think it's going to look great. And I promise I won't make you get the biggest tree in the lot."

"*Gut*. It would take up the whole gathering room."

"We can't have that. It's going to be hard enough to get it set up." He clapped his hands together. "How long is it going to take you to finish your inventory?"

Looking sheepish, she said, "I don't actually need to sort through all of this right now. I did a big shopping run right after Thanksgiving. Want to leave around ten?"

"Ten sounds perfect." He noticed that her eyes were glowing. For the first time since his arrival, she didn't look as if she was scared to face the day. "You know if we go look at trees, we might as well pick up a wreath, too."

She nodded. "I thought of that. And I would like to get some pretty red ribbon, too."

"You going to make a bow for the wreath?"

"*Nee*. But I do want to hang Christmas cards up on the walls." She smiled then, gifting him with a bit of her happiness. "*Danke*, Eric. I am looking forward to this."

"Me too. I can hardly wait."